TRANSMISSION ERROR

Borgo Press Books by MICHAEL KURLAND

Perchance: A Tale of the Paraverse
The Princes of Earth: A Science Fiction Novel
A Study in Sorcery: A Lord Darcy Novel
Ten Little Wizards: A Lord Darcy Novel
Transmission Error: A Scientifiction Romance
The Trials of Quintilian: Three Stories of Rome's Greatest Detective
The Unicorn Girl: An Entertainment
Victorian Villainy: A Collection of Moriarty Stories

TRANSMISSION ERROR

A SCIENTIFICTION
ROMANCE

MICHAEL KURLAND

THE BORGO PRESS
MMXII

Any resemblance between any characters or events in this book and your Great Aunt Tillie or that 'thing' that happened after your Senior Prom are blind luck and random chance, George.

TRANSMISSION ERROR

FIRST BORGO PRESS EDITION

Published by Wildside Press LLC

www.wildsidebooks.com

DEDICATION

To Love,

With Linda

CONTENTS

CHAPTER ONE

I sat alone in the booth nursing my empty shot-glass. "Well," I said, "do you want to hear about it, or don't you?"

"Sure, sure," the robotender said, slapping me gently on the back with a spongy claw. "That's what I'm here for. Let's hear all about it—again." It refilled the empty shot-glass and made a chirping noise to inform Central Accounts to deduct another eighty cents from what was left of my govdole check.

"Sarcasm doesn't befit a machine," I said loftily. "If you don't want to hear about it, you can always go somewhere else."

"Very funny," the robotender snarled. "You know bickety well I'm screwed to the wall of this bickety booth."

"Bickety?" I stared in astonishment at the bloodshot lens in the wall. "Bickety?"

"I know what I'm trying to say," the machine informed me, "but somehow it always comes out 'bickety'."

"That's a shame," I said. I looked down at the green fluid in the shot-glass. "Life plays funny tricks on all of us. Take my girl."

"What could I do with her?" the robotender asked, sounding interested.

"Nice girl," I said. "Lovely girl." I gulped the stuff down and felt it trying to burn its way through my chest. "Only she hates me." I put my head on the table. "I love her, but she hates me."

"Say!" the machine said. "Maybe I could spell it."

"What's that?" I looked up.

"Glerb," the robotender said. "Gluff. Bickety. What I'm

trying to say is spelled gak-thuggle-erk-erk-mfg. Oh, what's the bickety use?" It poured another shot of green gunk into my glass. "Here, this one's on me."

"Thanks," I said. "You know, it's not so much the way she said it as what she said."

"Perhaps you misunderstood," the robo-bickety-tender said.

"I doubt it. It was pretty unambish...unambiguous. What is this stuff?"

The robotender gestured with its mechanical arm. "On Ribbolar Three they heat their homes with it. On Earth they drink it. Like the man says: Call it what you want to and use it for the same purpose."

I looked at my glass with new respect. Ribbolar Djinn, so called because after the third shot a man could see the strangest things coming out of the bottle. "How many have I had?"

Another mechanical gesture. "Who's counting?"

"Thanks old pal. And who's going to carry me home?"

"Consider this your home," the mechanical fiend suggested. "What did the lady say?"

The visions were starting. Little blue men were coming in the door. I ignored them. No visions were going to freak me out. "She said, 'Daniel'—that's my name, Daniel—she said, 'Daniel, if you were the last man on Earth, I'd migrate.' That's what she said." I was feeling very sorry for myself. "Just cause I'm still on govdole and she's got a category three. Everyone knows it's easier for women to get jobs. I offered her my love and she spurned me." I blinked back a tear. My visions were getting closer. They had stopped at one of the other booths and were talking to the man inside. I wondered what he was drinking. It didn't seem fair, somehow, that he should have my visions.

"That's a shame," the robotender said. "A real shame. She shouldn't have said that. What's it like, being in love?"

"You wouldn't understand." The machine was getting more human every minute. I patted his chrome speaking panel. "Poor bickety robot. Never to know love. Never to feel the exquisite pain of being rejected. Never to get drunk and see little blue men. I feel sorry for you, old pal."

"It—" the robotender made a sound that was suspiciously like a sob. "It has its compensations. I might not be able to experience, but I can empathize. I was built with a large amount of empathy. I can empathize with two hundred and fifty-three people at once. Some of the stories that are in my memory banks would really increase your human understanding. Stories that should be told by a Faulkner, an O. Henry, a Service. Say, are you a writer? Listen, I could tell you the stories and you could write them down and polish them up a bit...."

"I'm not a writer," I said. "I'm just a govdole slob. Nobody loves ya when you're unemployed."

"That's a shame," the robot said. "Some of the stories I've heard." He snickered. "Some of the dirty jokes too. It's a shame I can't tell them. A bickety shame. That would cheer you up."

"Dirty jokes are jokes about sex," I told the robotender, "and right now nothing about sex could cheer me up. If I were the last man on Earth, I'd hit her right in the bickety." For some reason I thought that was funny. I put my head on the table and giggled. "Right in the bickety. You know, I used to have this fantasy. This dream, like; only I wasn't asleep. I used to imagine that I was the only man on Earth and the future of the Human Race depended on me—if you know what I mean. Well, I was going to get these girls and set up a...."

"Mister Godfrey?"

I looked up. My three blue men were gathered around my booth. Two of them were royal blue and the third was powder blue. They didn't look so little from close up. "Go away," I said.

"Mister Daniel C. Godfrey?"

"Listen," I said, shaking a finger at them. "I'm not used to being questioned by figments of my own imagination. Now go away. Unless your name is Marley. Is your name Marley?"

"I am Sergeant Biddle of the Eastcom Police. Are you Daniel C. Godfrey?" He sounded very annoyed for a figment. He was being polite, but I could tell it was a strain.

"That's my name." I put my two hands flat on the table and took a deep breath. The room started to spin a little faster. "What do you want?"

The powder-blue one spoke up. "According to paragraph three, section two, of Public Law three-one-six, a defendant is entitled to counsel from the moment of contact with the civil authorities," he said. But he ran all the words together, like they were memorized and he'd said them often. Accordingto-paragraphthreesectiontwoofPublicLawthree-one-six...."

Like that. "I am a court-appointed lawyer and will represent you until the termination of your case or until you obtain your own counsel. My name is Bogart." He paused for breath.

"What is this?" I asked. These figments were acting too real. I'd seen this scene played on the tridee many times, but never with me as the central character. For a second I thought it might be a simulife cast but I couldn't afford them. Besides, I'd remember putting the helmet on. Besides, I'd never pick this kind of role. The few times I've splurged on a simulife I've always picked heroic parts: knights in armor, cowboy heroes, stuff like that.

"Where were you at six o'clock this evening?" royal blue Sergeant Biddle asked.

"Well, I...."

"Defendant is not required to answer that question," powder-blue Bogart said. "He has not been informed of his rights. I advise him to remain mute." He looked at me. "That means don't say anything."

"It is my duty to inform you that you are suspected of being implicated in the murder of Alicia Grundel, and that anything you say may be used in evidence against you," Biddle said. He pushed a brass button on his blue jacket. "I am now recording. Case of the people Versus Daniel C. Godfrey in the matter of the death of Alicia Grundel. Suspect is being questioned on the premises of the Great Auk Saloon. Where were you at six o'clock in the evening of March twelve this year—that being tonight?"

My numbed brain had picked up one piece of information out of what they had said. "Alicia's dead?" I asked.

"On advice of counsel; attorney Laurence Bogart, license number 1C459236275, suspect declines to answer that question," Lawyer Bogart said clearly.

"How—?" I said. "Who—?"

"Miss Grundel is dead," Sergeant Biddle admitted. "Were you friendly with her?"

"On advice of counsel—" Bogart started.

"Wait a minute!" I yelped. "What's going on here?"

"Will you answer questions about the death of Alicia Grundel?" the Sergeant asked.

"I don't know anything about the death of...I didn't even knew she was.... My God!" I put my head down on the table and started to cry.

"On the advice of counsel, suspect is not answering any questions at this time," my powder-blue lawyer said.

"Then I'll have to take the suspect formally into custody." Sergeant Biddle said firmly. "Daniel Godfrey, I must take you in for questioning. Will you please come along with me." Sergeant Biddle and his silent partner helped me out of the booth and, with their hands firmly in my armpits, propelled me toward the door. Not that I was resisting; my legs just didn't seem to work. Lawyer Bogart scurried alongside.

"Goodbye," someone called. I turned my head. The robotender in my booth was waving a long, sad, mechanical claw at me. "Goodbye, old friend."

CHAPTER TWO

The policemen in the station were nice and polite when they booked me. They put me in a cozy cell and let me sleep off the Ribbolar Djinn before they questioned me. When I woke up Lawyer Bogart came in to see me. I told him what had happened the evening before, which information he insisted on referring to as "my story." He didn't seem to think it was much of a story, but agreed to let me tell it to the police. He told me we could always cop a plea, which made me very nervous.

Sergeant Biddle took me into a little room to question me. Bogart was there, and People's Attorney Mather, and a stenographer to operate the video recorder. We sat down around a table, and People's Attorney Mather smiled at me. He had a lot of teeth. "Just tell us what happened," he said.

"When?" I asked.

"When you killed Alicia Grundel," Mather suggested.

"I didn't," I said. Bogart had told me to give short answers.

"Did you see her around six o'clock last night?" Sergeant Biddle asked.

"Yes."

"What happened then?"

I shrugged. "We were supposed to go out for dinner. I was picking her up at the office since she was working late. She was a confidential secretary for Senator Ben Isaak von Turner."

"We know," People's Attorney Mather said, keeping the smile steady. "What time did you get there?"

"About quarter to six, I guess."

"You guess?"

"Well, anyhow, it was before six."

"What happened then?"

"I went into her office and she said she'd only be a minute finishing what she was doing; so I sat down to wait. We talked while she was finishing. Since it was just collating the pages of a report she'd typed up for the Senator, she didn't have to concentrate. The talk turned into an argument, and I got mad and walked out. That's what happened."

"Argument?" Smiley Mather asked. "You wouldn't call it a fight?"

"No." I shook my head. "Just an argument."

"Then how do you account for the fact that three people in the outer office heard your 'argument'?"

My lawyer had warned me about getting mad; so I didn't. "The walls are thin, and those secretaries are nosey."

"They say you were yelling at her."

"I might have done a little yelling," I admitted.

"What was the argument about?" Sergeant Biddle asked.

"Well," I tried to remember how it had started. It seemed so unimportant now. "She said we were going to dinner at the Four Horsemen. I said I couldn't afford it. She said she'd pay for it, I shouldn't worry. I said I'd damn well pay for our meal. She said then why didn't I get a job so I could afford to or stop letting my stupid pride get in the way. I said I was a trained cyberno technician and as soon as the lists opened up and my name came to the top I'd be earning a lot more than she was. She said that would take twenty years. I said it wouldn't, and besides, if it did then we'd just have to wait twenty years because I wasn't going to marry any woman and live off her salary. Then she said she wouldn't marry me if I were the last man on Earth if I was going to be so stubborn. That's when I walked out. There was a lot more in between, but that's the basic idea."

"Didn't you leave something important out?" Smiley asked.

"I don't think so."

"What about the Telamp?"

"The what?"

Smiley consulted a sheet of paper. "An eight pound, synthetic gemstone, solid-state telepathic amplifier, used by sensitives to direct and amplify their thought projections."

"You mean the white thing that looked like a crystal ball?"

"That's right," Smiley Mather agreed. "The thing."

"So that's what it was. What about it?"

"Well, for one thing, how did it get your fingerprints all over it?"

"It was delivered while I was there, and Alicia asked me to open the package. Neither of us knew what it was, and there was no note, so we left it on top of the file."

"That's all?"

"Yes." I tried not to let my irritation show.

"You didn't use it to bash her over the head in a fit of anger?"

"No, I didn't," I stood up and found that I was shaking all over. "Now listen, if you think that I—"

"Sit down," Sergeant Biddle said. I sat down.

"How do you account for the fact that your fingerprints are the only ones on the instrument in question?"

"I don't," I said. "That's your job. All I know is that I didn't hit Alicia with that or anything else!"

"Can you account for the fact that the secretaries in the outer office swear that no one entered the office after you left until a girl went in and found Miss Grundel's body?"

"No. I can't account for that fact either."

"I see," Mather said. "Tell me, how do you account for the fact that a heatgram of the room, taken when the body was discovered at six forty-live, shows that nobody but you and the dead girl had been in the room for at least an hour?"

I couldn't answer that. I had no idea of what the answer could be. All I knew was that I didn't kill Alicia. But it began to look as if I'd never be able to convince anyone else. Even my own lawyer thought I'd done it.

The trial was quick and efficient. They were very fair, but if I'd been on the jury I would have convicted me. Bogart kept advising me to cop a plea and plead guilty to a lesser charge like manslaughter, until the trial started and it was too late, but somehow I couldn't do it. I kept thinking something would turn up to show that I was innocent.

After all, I was innocent, and on the tridee something's always turning up at the last minute. Having the advantage of knowing that I didn't do it, I kept trying to figure out how it could have been done. The fingerprints were easy, of course, if you've ever read or watched mysteries. Regular gloves would have left smudges that would show up with modern techniques, but rubberoid gloves wouldn't. But I couldn't get around the girls in the outer office—unless one of them had done it, which I didn't think—or the heatgram.

The thing that made me mad was that either a telepathic sensitive or an enceloreader cyberno could have established my innocence, but both were strictly illegal to use in court. As far as I could see it was another case where the law protected only the guilty, but the statutes against privacy invasion were very strict.

I had a few bad moments when I realized that, in a way, I was responsible for her death. If we hadn't had that stupid fight she would have gone out with me and she'd still be alive. They couldn't find the report she'd been collating, and for some reason the jury seemed to find that another point against me. To me it just proved that someone must have been in the room after I left. I knew it was a special report for Senator Turner and the Alien Culture Regulatory Committee, which he was chairman of.

I asked Bogart to get Senator Turner to testify, but he said that was silly. I insisted and he told me that Senator Turner had been killed in a scooter accident about an hour before Alicia was murdered. I said that proved something. Bogart wanted to know what, and I told him that I had no idea and he was my lawyer why didn't he figure it out. He said he thought he could still make a deal with the People's Attorney if I'd plead guilty. I refused.

I was found guilty of what the crime buffs call Murder Two, unpremeditated, and sentenced to be transported for life.

CHAPTER THREE

This transportation business is what I'd call a sneaky way to colonize the Galaxy. Admitted that Earth and some of the older planets are miserably overcrowded. Admitted that the good places can pick and choose who they want. I'd tried to talk Alicia into moving with me to one of the planets that needed good cyberno techs but she didn't want to give up her job, and having any job on Earth is more of a status symbol than being president of a lot of places. Now that I was a convicted felon, of course, I had no choice. I'd go to whatever hellhole they sent me and do prison work for twenty years. Then I'd be released to make my own way, free as a bird—as long as I stayed on that planet. With time off for good behavior, I might even get out of prison in seven years, but I'd still spend the rest of my life on that planet. Hell of a prospect.

I was taken to a large building somewhere and put through an indoctrination course with several hundred other felons. As usual, they were very polite. They told us of the good we'd be doing, and of the Noble Cause of spreading Humanity through the Galaxy. I couldn't see why they bothered at first, then I realized that most of the people—excuse me, felons—there were volunteers who had chosen transportation rather than spend years in one of Earth's overcrowded prisons.

After two weeks we were ready to leave. We were all lined up, given numbers, and told to count off in threes. We did.

"Okay, youse mens," the guard shouted at us through his megaphone, "the transmatter can only take youse three at a time, so youse'll have to be patient. Stay with your dropmates; youse'll all get your chance." We all thanked him loudly, but he ignored it. Three by three we approached the transmatter room and our chance for a new life.

The man in front of me in the lineup turned to me and stuck his hand out while we waited for the line to move. "My name's Long Harry. Looks like we'll be together for the drop."

"Daniel," I told him, looking up at his chin and the craggy face it supported. I'm just exactly six feet tall, and I seldom meet anyone who's a head taller than I am—and twice as wide. I was prepared for a bone-crushing grip, but his handshake was firm but delicate the way a careful man might hold a thin-stemmed glass.

"Ah, Daniel," he said. "I will forbear biblical puns, however appropriate they might seem at the moment. It will be a pleasure to drop with you, Daniel."

"I've heard," I told Long Harry, "that it isn't a pleasure to drop—alone or with company."

"The transmatter device does cause a momentary surge of discomfort," friend Harry admitted, "but think how tedious colonizing the Galaxy would be if it had to be done by ship."

"If the way it were to be done were left to me," the man behind me declared, "it would be by voluntary choice. I've a bit of business on this fine planet of my birth that I'd like a chance to finish before they drop me through the void." There was a musical lilt to his voice that emphasized the meaning of what he said.

Long Harry reached his large hand around me and extended it. "Ah, the third member of our involuntary chowder and drop-ping society. My name's Long Harry, and this here's Daniel."

"I heard you," the man said sourly. He was very small, barely five feet high; thin to the point of emaciation; with a large head, almost bald, which sported a pair of dark, glittering eyes and the largest, most angular nose I'd ever seen. His pallid complexion made a good attempt at blending in with the grey of the prison jumper he was wearing.

After a second's hesitation, he took the offered hand and shook it in one firm up-and-down motion. Then he did the same with mine. "You'll excuse my hesitation," he said. "I'm a very friendly man when I'm not preoccupied with black thoughts of things undone. A destiny that's mine to mold is being left in other hands. And I have—" here he paused and looked sharply at each of us before continuing "—other business here." It occurred to me that he couldn't be one of the volunteers if he felt that strongly about leaving, but it's impolite to ask a fellow felon what he got caught doing. "Daniel," he said. "Long Harry. They call me The Beak."

"It will be a pleasure to share a planet with you," Harry assured him. The line moved a bit forward, and we shuffled our mite toward the drop room. I could make out the hum of electronic gadgetry that came from behind the twin green doors labeled MATTER TRANSMISSION SUBUNIT: *Passenger and Cargo Station*. Below the sign, at the center of each door, was the trademark logo of the Transmatter Corporation: a pair of linked circles with a lightning bolt disappearing into one circle and coming out of the other.

The Beak stared mournfully at the doors as we approached them. When we finally reached them, and stood outside waiting to be called next, he ran his hands over the logo. "You know what this is?" he asked us. "A pair of electrified handcuffs."

"Come on now," Harry said, putting a large hand on our friend's shoulder, "it could be worse. Think of the punishments mankind has inflicted on its criminals during the long climb upward toward the light of civilization."

"Yes, I do," The Beak said sadly. "In ancient Greece the worst penalty, considered worse than death itself, was to be banished from the land. To be still alive, but never to set eyes on Athens again. To live among those who by their very speech were called barbarians—that was true punishment. And we are leaving Earth itself."

Harry said, "I'd call that a chauvinistic attitude, if you asked me. There are many planets I'd as soon live on as this one. I admit we're probably not going to one of those, but for me it's still better than spending the next twenty years of my life in a prison here on Mother Earth. What do you think, Daniel?"

I shrugged. "There's a power greater than my own that decides my fate," I said.

"Are you a believer?" Long Harry asked in surprise.

"I was referring," I informed him coldly, "to the prison authority."

The door opened and a green-smocked tech stuck his head out. "Next group, please." We went in. The room was large and square and filled with all sorts of machinery and electronic and protonic control devices. The only things I could identify with any feeling of confidence were the banks of computer cyberno sections, with their panels of readout lamps blinking in undulant confusion as the unit kept track of the relative positions of all the other transmatter stations on this net Any transmatter station can drop to all other transmatter stations, the only catch being that the sending unit has to know exactly where the receiving unit is. Anybody who makes a drop to a sloppily figured set of coordinates either will end up at any other station, apparently at random, or won't end up anywhere at all. The percentage of drops that just disappear is statistically insignificant—unless you happen to be about to make a drop yourself.

"Gentlemen," a tech in a red smock with the stripe of command around his sleeve addressed us, "would you be good enough to enter the Transmatter Development Stage, and we'll get under way."

"What you mean, we, white man?" The Beak muttered. We climbed into the drop cage and stood there, like three mice at a biologist's convention. The techs, in their smocks of office: white, red, green, blue or yellow according to section, went efficiently about the final checkout. The bored voice of the controller called off the list.

"Weight check."

"Two-three-five-two-seven-six grams."

"Parameters."

"Established. Point zero-five."

"Wave blank."

"Neutral."

"Rotation."

Point by point the checkout went on, and we mice stood mute, each occupied with his own thoughts. A small knot of fear established itself in my stomach and sent out exploratory runners to the rest of my body. Some people, I remember thinking, do this for fun.

"Contact."

"Contact firm."

"Automatic cycle."

"Starting. Ten seconds from.... Now!" A loud *bleep* sounded. Then another. The voice counted bleeps. "Eight...seven...six...." I could feel the beads of cold sweat gathering on my forehead. Fear of the unknown is always the greatest fear. "Three...two...."

Someone yelled "Break! Break!" and the tech in red jabbed for a button.

He didn't make it.

As the room faded out all the men in colored smocks were standing up and looking shocked.

I knew it.

* * * * * * *

I was falling in a tight spiral into myself, and the rest of the universe had disappeared. There was nothing but black, and fear, and what would have been nausea if I had a body. The drop was supposed to take only a moment, and the dropper wasn't supposed to be aware of the interval. This was taking forever, and I was very aware of it. *We missed*, I thought. *This is limbo, and I'll be here forever.*

"THE GAME IS OVER."

The alien thought came not as language, but as an idea unit.

Who are you? I thought. *What game?*

"NOT QUITE. THERE ARE
STILL A FEW PIECES TO PLAY."

Hello! Can you hear-feel-sense me? Who is it?

"YOU MUST LOSE."

"PERHAPS, BUT WE SHALL PLAY IT OUT."

Who—or what—ever they were, they weren't aware of me.

Things seemed to harden around me, and suddenly my body returned. I was lying, in a curled-up position, on a cold, dusty cement floor.

Someone sneezed.

CHAPTER FOUR

"God bless you," I said.

"Thanks," Long Harry answered, "but it was you that sneezed."

We were on a small, cement platform in the middle of a poorly-lit room which seemed to be constructed out of rough black stone. The light was coming-through randomly-placed chinks in the stone. Overhead were some squarish-looking pipes from which was coming the rattling sound of crushed ice in a cocktail shaker—only twenty times as loud.

"Friends," The Beak called. "I would not presume to give you instruction for the world—whatever world this is—but for myself, I consider it advisable to quit this platform in haste." He was standing in a corner of the chamber, his back to two walls, brandishing a length of pipe he had picked up somewhere. Here was a gentleman with a quick mind and fast reflexes—and the firm conviction that the Universe was out to get him.

Long Harry and I scrambled off the platform and into several inches of dust.

"Phew!" I said. "Careful kicking up the dust in here or we'll suffocate."

"Don't light a match," Long Harry added.

"I don't have a match," I told him. "Where are we?"

The Beak lowered his club and came out of the corner, suspiciously glancing around. "It would seem we're not wherever it was we were being sent."

The ice suddenly stopped rattling through the pipes. "What

was that?" The Beak yelled, spinning around.

Long Harry pointed an explanatory finger upward. "The bowling alley upstairs just closed for the night."

"Ah," The Beak said. "Then the machine has shut down."

"Machine?" I asked.

"And just how do you think we got here?"

"The transmatter upgefucked, obviously." I said. "It threw us here instead of Hellhole III, or wherever we were heading."

"Right-O. But 'here' has to be another transmatter portal. One cannot receive without a receiver, it's the third law of similarity."

"I wonder," Long Harry said, running his hand along the stone wall, "Who would put a transmatter in a place like this."

"Ask it," The Beak suggested. "You know what's a nice machine like you.... Ah! There's the control bank." He trotted over to the far wall and peered at the black stone. "That's funny, it doesn't look right."

"What's wrong with it?" Long Harry asked.

"Here," I said, "let me look. I'm a trained cyberno tech."

"If there's anything I can't stand," The Beak said, "it's a More Competent, Better Informed Than Thou attitude; but have a look."

I looked. It was wrong. It was all wrong, with the same sense of alienness as the Easter Island statues or the glyphs on Deimos. The controls and indicators—and I couldn't tell which were which or even if that's what they were—were arranged along the border of a three-foot hexagram. Three smooth, black triangular panels were spaced inside the diagram.

Long Harry grinned. "Well?"

"It doesn't look right," I agreed. "Let's not touch it."

"The furthest thing from my mind," Long Harry assured me. "How do we get out of here?"

"It would. appear that *that's* a door," the Beak said, pointing to a patch of deeper black across the room.

"How can you tell?" Long Harry asked, looking doubtfully in the indicated direction.

"I have an infallible sense of exit," The Beak said. "But I promise not that what lies waiting beyond yon portal bodes us good."

"Someday when I know you better," Long Harry said, "I'll have to remember to ask where you learned to talk like that. But for now, we might as well see whether what lies outside is edible."

"Or whether it considers us edible," The Beak added darkly.

The door, at least, was sensible. It had a handle. A large, square handle, true; but, nonetheless a handle. Long Harry turned it until there was a click and the door rose smoothly into the ceiling.

"Hrumph!" Long Harry said, staring up at the gloom. He added a few precise curse words, and finished off with, "hrumph-ha!"

"Very nice," The Beak said. "I must remember to ask you where you picked up your vocabulary."

The room beyond the rising door was long and narrow and twisted off to the left. We went along it Indian-file; Long Harry took the lead and I brought up the middle.

"We seem to be going down," Long Harry commented.

"We are going down," The Beak affirmed. "I only hope nothing's coming up." On that cheerful note we continued along the twisty corridor.

"Oof!" Long Harry said firmly.

"What?" I said, bumping into him. "Why have you stopped?"

"Because the hallway has. There's a door in front of me."

"Where does it go?" I asked.

"You tell me."

"Open it," The Beak suggested. "And get off my foot."

"Sorry," I said, stepping gingerly sideways. "I can't see."

"I can't either, but I'm not on your foot."

"Stop bickering," Long Harry said. "There's noises outside."

"Noises?" I said. "Noises?"

"Stop stuttering," The Beak said. "What sort of noises?"

"Put your ear to the door and listen for yourself," Long Harry invited. "I can't tell." The three of us crowded against the door and listened. There was a muted roaring sound with choppy overtones just audible through the panel.

"It sounds like the ocean," I said.

"Well that answers one question," Long Harry said. "The door's made out of seashells."

"It feels like some sort of metal," I said.

"Don't be silly," Long Harry explained. "Everyone knows that you only hear the ocean if you put your ear to a seashell."

I had a feeling Long Harry was somehow disappointed with me.

"It sounds like the wind rushing through trees, with just a trace of rain," The Beak offered. "Could be, perhaps, a summer shower."

"It's too loud," Long Harry said. "Well, only one way to find out." He twisted the handle and this door too slid up and disappeared into the ceiling.

I was blinded by sunlight and deafened by a tremendous roar.

CHAPTER FIVE

My eyes adjusted as we stepped out of the doorway. We were on a kind of square balcony, with the building behind us and steps going down the other three sides. All was of the same rectangular blocks of light-grey stone. Along the building wall, on both sides of the doorway, were ornamental racks of long, ornate spears; wrapped and tufted with varicolored cloth.

In front of us, down the steps, was a cleared sandy area about twice the size of a football field as seen from one of the goalposts. Surrounding the football field was the stadium.

We were in an arena.

The loud roaring sound was the screaming of the assembled multitude. It was games day at the coliseum.

The score of the current match seemed to be Lions two, Christians nothing. Only they weren't Lions (or, as it turned out, Christians). Two very human-looking corpses were distributed about the field. The rest of the squad, a group of very tattered-looking humans, were in slow retreat behind fixed spears.

The monster they were retreating from might have been many things, but it was not a lion. It might have been two pythons from the necks up. In trunk and leg it might have been a rhinoceros; and in tail, an alligator. Surrounding the double-python neck, right where it joined the rhino body, was a thick, varicolored ruff that changed in hue faster than you could watch. As the beast lumbered across the field its two tiny heads, each about half the size of a man, but small in relation to its bulk, jabbed from side to side and snapped their beaks, producing a sound like a volley of pistol fire, which could be heard clearly above the crowd.

"What in hell is that?" Long Harry asked.

"I never dream in color," The Beak assured us. "And my nightmares are of a more personal nature."

"This isn't one of mine," I said. "This is real, whatever it is."

"We are agreed, gentlemen, that it isn't a dream," Long Harry said dryly. "Have you noticed that the door has closed behind us?"

I turned and saw that the door had dropped silently back into place. With a short expletive of regret, I leaped for the handle and twisted, but it refused to budge.

"I already tried," Long Harry told me. "I'm afraid we're stuck."

"Stuck it is," The Beak said, as though he had expected no less.

The roaring of the crowd got louder. The three victims were backed up against one of the walls and, as the monster calmly surveyed his lunch, one of them was attempting a counterattack. Holding his spear above his head, he ran forward and thrust the nine-foot pig sticker savagely at the nearest head. The head jerked back, as surprised as I would be if a hamburger tried to bite. With an air of gentle persuasion, the serpent head caught the spear in its beak and twisted up, pulling it out of the man's hand like an asp munching on a toothpick, it chewed the thing up and spat out wood pulp. Then it gently nudged the man with the back of its head, sending him flying twenty feet to slam up against the arena wall. He slid down to the packed earth and lay still, a crumpled mass.

Stomping its collective feet and cheering wildly, the crowd applauded.

The beast's spare head suddenly lifted up inquisitively and fixed its gaze. It was staring straight at us.

"Swell," The Beak said. "Good-oh! I was afraid we were going to be ignored."

The monster stood frozen in indecision. One head glowered

down at the two people cowering against the wall, while the other cocked slowly to the side as it stared at us.

"Well, what now?" I asked, trying to make myself as inconspicuous as I could against the side of the building.

"I couldn't say, I really couldn't say," The Beak said. "I'm only on lesson five. Now if this were the mythical hippocamele-lephantoleopardus, we could disperse him with the powder of finely ground unicorn horn or dispatch him with an arrow dipped in virgin's milk; if we had either a unicorn or a lactating virgin. "*Monsters, comma, general nonspecific, comma, removal of,* is lesson seven. Sorry."

The audience, following the monster's gaze, was beginning to notice us. Their roar died down to a murmur and their murmur to a whisper; then they shut up entirely. Straight across from us, on the far side of the arena, was a small area covered by a muddy-yellow canopy. In it sat what must be the local equivalent of royalty. Four or five of the richly-robed group were engaged in an animated discussion which, judging by their gestures, concerned us. I couldn't decide whether this was a good or bad sign. The Beak offered the opinion that half the group were holding out for our immediate execution, while the rest were insisting we be tortured first for desecrating their temple.

"What makes you think it's a temple?" Long Harry asked.

"It's always a temple," The Beak explained.

The monster decided first. With a warning snap at its lunch to behave themselves while it was gone, it trotted across the dirt toward us.

Long Harry wrenched one of the spears from its ornamental support and handed it to me. "Aim at the throat," he commented.

"Which one?" I asked, resenting, the calm with which he faced what I regarded as a silly way to die. I have always favored extreme old age.

Ignoring me, he loosened two more monster-stickers and handed one to The Beak, who hefted it determinedly.

As armies learned long ago, the thing that makes most men march into battle instead of turning and running is neither patriotism nor fear of their noncoms; although both of these play their small part. It is mainly the fact that men would rather die than look foolish in front of their friends. This is why soldiers, as much as possible, train with the units they're sent to fight in.

From the neck down I wanted to run. The fact that there was no place to run had nothing to do with it; if I faced this monster it was going to kill me, if I ran long enough it might trip and break its neck—necks—chasing me.

My forebrain securely in control, I stood there hefting the spear, with a vicious warscowl on my face, cursing myself for being too cowardly to run.

The spear was about ten feet long, of some smooth, close-grained, dark wood; tipped by a large iron barb. It weighed about half a ton. My best guess was that I could hold it upright for about three minutes; I wasn't sure if I could manage to thrust with it at all.

The ground vibrated as the monster lumbered across the field, picking up momentum. Both heads were arched toward us, beaks snapping in pistol-shot unison. The crowd continued silent except for some shouting and gesturing from scattered individuals.

"They're taking bets," Long Harry said, with the air of one knowledgeable in such fields. "I wonder what the odds are."

I knew which side I'd take, but I decided not to say. A horn blew, and the crowd swiveled to look at the royal box. One man stood up in it and gestured toward ground level.

Diddly-pom, pheep pheep
Diddly-pom, pheep, pheep
Diddly pom, pheep, fiddle-faddle, pheep, pheep, pheep.
A group of red-clad men at the foot of the royal box had picked up various pieces of ironmongery and were producing noises with them. The effect was that of a high-school band attempting a piece it didn't know with a variety of wrong sheet music and a deaf leader with a drinking problem.

"Well, well," The Beak said, "we get a dirge."

The monster picked up its heads at the sound of the music.

Its feet went into step with the rhythm, then it slowed down and stopped entirely about sixty feet from the steps. Heads undulating happily, it sat down. "Reprieve," I sighed, leaning on my spear.

"Music hath charm...," Long Harry said.

"Let's attack it while it's down," The Beak suggested.

"That's not sporting," Long Harry said.

"Sporting!" The Beak snorted.

"From their point of view. They might turn the beast back on. Let's trust fate. After all, we did come out of a building, which you say is a temple, that they thought was empty. Maybe they think we're gods, or something."

"It's probably the 'or something'," The Beak commented. "Perhaps they get all their victims through the same sort of transmission error that brought us here. Besides, what better way to test a god than to see if yon monster can shred him into godbites. Gods are supposed to be immortal."

"Not all gods," Long Harry said. "We've had a couple that weren't."

"Please," I said. "Couldn't we have a theological discussion some other time?"

"Maybe you have something better to talk about?" The Beak asked. "Contemporary art, perhaps. You like Neo-Abstract Realism, or do you prefer Brightilistic Suppression?"

"What about 'Levitation for the Millions'?" I suggested. "Or, 'The Art of Invisibility'?"

The beast still swayed, the musicians still played, and the crowd under the canopy still argued.

"Can you sing?" Long Harry asked.

"That's an idea, let's form a choral group," I said.

"As a matter of fact, that is the idea. Can you sing?"

The Beak said; "I know some old Scottish war ballads."

"No, I mean something we all know. Do you know any bleep?"

"I hate modern music," I said.

"That's a big help. What about stuff from five or ten years

ago? Everyone picks up songs when he's in school."

"I guess I could dig some songs out of my memory," I admitted. "What's the idea?"

The trumpet sounded again, and the music stopped. You could have heard a pin drop anywhere in the stadium. You could have heard a curse word from me as I dropped my spear back to the ready. The royal box must have decided against us.

"Quiet," Long Harry whispered. "It may have forgotten us."

It hadn't.

With the lulling influence of the music gone, the savage beast stopped swaying. All four little red eyes gleamed and the pair of beaks started a castanet crescendo. The rhythmic quivering that had been chasing up and across the beast's thick hide died out, and it broke into a lumber.

"Gilbert and Sullivan," Long Harry said urgently.

We did *Pinafore* in high school," I remembered; raising my spear. "Also *The Mikado*. I was a spear carrier.

"I remember *Mikado*," The Beak said. "Fine. Excellent."

The beast had reached the foot of the stairs, and was starting up.

"This thing likes music," Long Harry barked, "so let's give it some. *A Wandering Minstrel* on three."

"Right," I said.

"It won't work," The Beak said.

"Sue me in the next world," Long Harry told him. "One, two, three!"

"*A wandering minstrel I,*" I croaked. One of the heads was now slightly above me glaring down, its beak moving from side to side. "*A thing of rags and patches. Of ballad songs and snatches.*"

We were all singing now.

"*...and dreamy lullabies,*" the Beak roared, slashing at a descending snake's head with the tip of his spear.

We were in a tight group against the wall, spears pointing outward in three directions against the beast that surrounded us. "*My catalogue is long through every passion ranging,*" we harmonized, "*and to your humor changing....*"

The heads started to sway slightly. "*I tune my supple song.*"

The swaying increased. One set of red eyes closed. "*Are you in a sentimental mood? I'll sigh with you, Oh sorrow, sorrow.*"

The other head took The Beak's spear gently out of his hands and munched it in time with our singing. A moist film covered the eyes, and then they too closed. Sine waves rippled down the creature's armored back.

"*On maiden's coldness do you brood? I'll do so too, Oh, sorrow, sorrow.*"

"What now," The Beak whispered; the two massive heads beating time over us.

"Keep singing," Long Harry instructed. "*I'll charm your willing ears....*"

Leaving The Beak and me to our operatic duet, Long Harry stalked toward the point of the undulating V formed by the creature's necks.

"*...with songs of lover's fears.*"

Inserting the tip of his spear carefully between the necks, he pushed. Nothing happened. He pushed harder.

"*With sympathetic tears my cheeks bedew. Oh sorrow!*"

A gush of bright purple liquid spurted over the steps. The beast shuddered and sixty pounds of snake neck hit me on the head. I fell, and one of the heads landed right beside me. The creature let out a dying gasp. Its breath smelled of marsh gas and rotten fruit. My stomach turned over and just barely decided to stay where it was.

"Come on," The Beak said, pulling me to my feet. "Thanks to Saint George here, I think we're heroes."

CHAPTER SIX

The band started playing, the trumpets sounded, the people cheered, and a troop of soldiers in gleaming brass armor marched on the field to escort us out. We double-timed once around the arena to the squeal of a dozen trumpets (to me anything that's brass and blown through to produce noise is a trumpet), paused to pick up the two survivors of the beast's first attacks, and dog-trotted off the field. Behind us a cleanup squad was policing the bodies.

A large gate in the arena wall was cranked up as we approached it and then dropped back down as soon as the last soldier had passed through, leaving us in a square, flat area with high stone walls and a dirt floor. A pair of brick tunnel entrances with iron-barred gates were at the far end.

The troop of soldiers snapped to attention and their leader did a fancy sword-flourish salute aimed at the top of the wall. A crowned head was peering cautiously over the side and staring at us. It stared for a long moment and then disappeared, to be replaced by two hooded, mustached heads. After a minute's intense staring, they went into a murmured dialog and then the one on the left barked an order and they both retreated out of sight.

The sword flourish was repeated to the empty wall, the leader yelled a variant of the order, and we marched toward one of the brick tunnels. The iron bars were raised at our approach, and a sub-squad of men detached themselves from the main body and marched us and the two survivors into the tunnel.

We ended up in a large, stone room that had been barred off into a corridor and many cells. The five of us were prodded into a corner cell and left. Except for us, the room was empty.

The favorite writing exercise when I was in grade school, right after, "My Summer Vacation," which, after all, is only good once a year, was, "Describe a Room." I was never very fond of that. While the other kids would wax on about "Grandma's Kitchen," which was always full of the odor of Grandma's cooking and strong with her Unspoken Presence—gingham mats and calico potholders and jars full of homemade preserves and other esoterica—my mind would go blank. I would end up with something that read like a blueprint: "This room, on the northeast corner of the house, is twelve feet long and ten feet wide. The door is two feet from the left corner. The ceiling is ten feet high, with a molding two feet from the top. There are three windows...."

Like that.

This room I could have described; look, smell, sound, touch, even the taste. It was distinctive. It was unique. It was depressing and horrible. We were there for two days. They went like this:

Our cell was about six feet wide by fifteen feet long. Since we were in a corner cell, two of the sides were stone walls while the opposite two were iron bars. The long barred side adjoined the next cell, while the six-foot side faced the corridors and had the small door we had been shoved through. The ceiling was stone, and covered with a green mold which appeared to undulate softly in the dim light provided by oil lamps set every few yards in high niches in the walls. I tried estimating the height of the ceiling by timing the droplets of freezing water which formed on the rough stone and fell onto the layer of straw covering the dirt floor, but I got a different answer each time I did. It was at least fourteen feet. The straw, which was knee deep in places, hadn't been changed since the place was built. A new layer was added from time to time to cover the compacted, rotting mass beneath. To add to the joy, the rats—they looked like Earth rats, even if they were the size of terriers—had their tunnels in the compacted straw.

When we were first thrust into the cell we gathered, Long Harry, The Beak, and I, by the bars and watched our captors march away. Our other two guests immediately dropped on the straw in back of the cell and passed out.

"Very nice, this is," The Beak said disgustedly, staring out the bars. "Heroes we are. A fine thing."

I sat down on the damp straw and leaned back against the bars. "Well, that settles it; they don't think we're gods."

"The first thing," Long Harry said, pacing back and forth and raising a cloud of fine grit as he walked, "is to figure out how to get out of here. Whatever they have in mind for us, I don't think we'll like it."

"While I think of it," I said, "before I get too depressed; you did a fine job on that beast. That was quick thinking and cool fighting."

"Thank you, Daniel. It's elementary strategy. Always remember that the best defense is a quick right to the jaw."

"Argh!" The Beak said. "Rats!" For a second I thought it was a comment on Long Harry's dictum, but then a fat, grey shape scuttled into the cell, darted over my outstretched legs and disappeared into the straw. Several more raced down the corridor to disappear into various cells.

Their hurry to get clear of the corridor was quickly explained. The sound of distant thunder shook the room, getting louder and louder, and then a monster beast boomed into view at the far end of the corridor and thumped his way past us and out of sight. It was a minute before the ground stopped shaking. This was a different creature than the one we fought. Larger than an Earth elephant, it looked like a cross between an armadillo and a World War One tank.

"Well," Long Harry said, pulling at his ear, "this is the gangway for the menagerie—very interesting."

"I think someone should take a look at our companions over there," The Beak said. "Find out what shape they're in, if any." He squatted by the two figures stretched out on the straw and peered at them with professional concern. "This one's pretty well knocked about. I've no joining and mortising supplies with me, but we'll make what repairs we can." With surprising gentleness he peeled the tattered robe from the unconscious man's blood-matted skin and set about cleaning and binding. the wounds. At his instruction I set about finding the freshest straw I could.

Long Harry wandered over to take a look. "Do you think they're human?"

"As far as I can tell," The Beak told him. "Not only that, but we've got one of each."

"One of each what?" Long Harry asked.

"Sex. This one's a girl."

This one was indeed a girl. Having finished binding up her companion, an old man with a wispy, white beard, The Beak was sponging her face off with the cleanest damp straw I could find him. She looked to be no more than sixteen; the face of an angel, marked by the slight remains of adolescent skin trouble. Her body beneath the robe (well, we had to clean and bandage her wounds, didn't we?) had the well-proportioned muscular look of an athlete—say a swimmer or dancer.

We tried to make both of them as comfortable as possible. The girl tossed about and groaned a lot, and occasionally she'd let off a scream, or a string of words we couldn't understand. The Beak said this was a sign she was getting over her shock and exhaustion, and she'd probably be all right after she got some sleep. The old man just lay there without moving, getting whiter and whiter. I didn't need The Beak to tell me this was bad, but there wasn't anything we could do. When a chill wind started blowing through the corridor—which Long Harry said meant it was night outside; I didn't know, having spent most of my life in a climate-controlled city—we took off our prison-denim jackets and covered the old man and the girl as best we could.

A while later a guard came through and tossed a hunk of soggy bread through the bars at us. We tried to find some way of telling him that there was a very sick man in the cell. He conveyed to us with an elaborate shrug that he didn't understand, and if he did he wouldn't care.

"Phaugh!" The Beak said, squatting by the bars and poking through them with a long stick he had found. "By a tremendous stroke of luck, we have succeeded in exchanging one prison for another several orders of magnitude worse then the original."

"This might have its advantages," Long Harry told him. "Try to relax and hang cool for a while."

"Cool is the right word," The Beak said.

I agreed.

A second warder came through then carrying a long stick with a cap at the end. He went from oil lamp to oil lamp, snuffing them out, trailing gloom behind him. The last lamp went out, and we could hear his quickened footsteps as he went back down the corridor and the scurry of little feet as our grey neighbors took advantage of the dark. The warder broke out into a run, and his footsteps clattered down the corridor for quite a way.

"Damn fool's afraid of rats," Long Harry said.

"You don't have to be a damn fool to be afraid of rats," I said, squeezing myself tighter into my corner.

"No," Long Harry admitted, "but you have to be a damn fool to put out lights down to the far end, instead of from the far end back, if you are."

He had a point.

"Well, what are we going to do?" The Beak asked.

"Well indeed. We'll have a conference now to discuss ways of getting out of here. I think I have an idea," said Long Harry.

"Let's do it in the morning, I'm too tired," I said, and promptly fell asleep. The discussion may have gone far into the night, but somehow I doubt it.

I was first up the next morning. The lights had already been turned back on, and a bundle of clean straw had been shoved into a corner of the cell. Prison reform is a wonderful thing.

My cellmates were wakened shortly by a stampede of horned

and plated creatures that rumbled through the corridor, weaving from side to side and banging against the iron bars as they locomoted across the room. The Beak cursed and threw a clot of straw at them, but Long Harry rose to a cross-legged position and stared speculatively at the beasts.

"What are you thinking," I asked him, "and will it get us out of here?"

"And a good morning to you, too," he said. "I was just thinking that a cup of coffee would go very nicely about now."

"Indeed," The Beak agreed. "A cup of coffee, and about five pounds of plastic explosive."

The girl was also awake now. She had retreated to the far end of the cell and was sitting huddled in the corner, as though trying to get as far away from us as possible in the tiny cell. Considering what we looked like, I really couldn't blame her.

"Don't be afraid, small one," Long Harry said. He broke off a piece of what was left of last night's bread. "Here, have a bit of healthy, slightly-damp bread. It will do you good." He extended the bread toward her, so she would know what he meant. She reached out for it, took it, and retreated back to her corner. She was looking at us now with an expression of shock that I didn't understand. We looked bad, all right, but not *that* bad.

"Maybe the judge what tried me is right," The Beak said, noting the girl's expression. "We are feral tigers that must be isolated from civilization, we are. The girl can tell it just from looking at us." He went over and knelt beside the old man, checking for a pulse in the thin wrist. He pried the eyelid back and then pushed his thumbnail into the old man's cheek. "Dead," he announced. "Departed of his existence several hours ago. Would you like your coats back?"

Long Harry calmly took his denim jacket and put it back on. I did my best to match his nonchalance; after all, I was a convicted murderer.

"Dead?"

We turned and stared. It was the girl. "What was that?" I asked, feeling foolish.

"Dead?" Her brown eyes focused on mine, and large tears formed in their corners. "Matlos is dead?"

"You speak English?"

Long Harry snorted. "Now if that isn't the brightest question ever. That's a winner, that is. Do you speak English! You'll have to excuse him, young lady; he must have had a touch of the sun back in the arena. What he meant was, 'You speak English well,' or 'How is it that you speak English?' or perhaps, 'Where did you learn English?'"

"English?" the girl asked.

Long Harry looked suspiciously at me, and then back at the girl. "The language you're speaking now is commonly known as English."

"You call the sacred language English? How did it get such an odd name among your people? You are priests of Tor the Mighty aren't you? From some far distant and uncivilized part of the globe? How else could you have learned the sacred language? Is Matlos really dead? It's all right, I'm a priestess of the second order; really I am. These barbarians stole my Amulet of Rank and Authority when they captured us. Matlos couldn't really be dead, after having come so far and survived so much. It would be too cruel. English? No, I'll be all right. I'm trying not to cry, really I am; but it's hard. Talk to me for a minute, please. It was such a shock to hear you speak the sacred language. I was quite frightened for a minute. But I'll be all right now." She paused, and her breath came quickly, and then she burst into racking sobs, drawing her knees up to her chest and rocking back and forth.

The Beak sat in the straw beside her and smoothed her hair with the tender, awkward concern of a man who is unable to shield his daughter from the universe and doesn't know how to tell her. "The old man is dead," he said. "He died quietly during the night. I'm sorry."

The girl spoke haltingly, trying not to cry between words. "I'm sorry too. We didn't even know each other before we were captured. We were on the same ship, is all. He tried to take care of me, and I tried to take care of him. And I'm alive, and he's dead. I'm sorry, I'm so sorry."

The Beak took her in his arms and they rocked back and forth and he said soothing things to her, but the expression in his face didn't change, it was as hard as ever.

Long Harry squatted by the front of the cell, his large fist wrapped around one of the bars. "We're all prisoners here together, for some unspecified crime. I wonder if we'll get to see a judge, or if sentence has already been passed."

The girl looked up. "Prisoners? We're slaves. I thought you knew. We'll either go back in the arena or be sold at auction. That is, you will; I'll probably be put in one of the soldiers' houses. I'd rather go back to the arena."

"I should have guessed," Long Harry said. He stared speculatively at the bars for a minute, and then asked the girl, "What's your name?"

"Thalla."

"Don't worry about a thing, Thalla. We're going to get out of here tonight. Are you with us?"

"Oh yes—but how?"

"I have a scheme. Listen, if I get us out of here, can you direct us to some place safe?"

"There won't be any place in the city that's safe," Thalla said, "but I think I can get us out of the city without too much trouble. This is a central point for pimpadigrots—caravans—and I should be able to get us work on one. The masters aren't very picky."

"I assume the local language isn't English," The Beak said.

"Oh no," Thalla said, "the sacred language is only known to Servants of Tor. Or, at least, I thought the sacred language was only known...."

"That's a problem," Long Harry said. "We don't know the language or the customs. We'll stand out like a trio of sore thumbs."

"No problem," Thalla said. "There are so many foreigners in Grak, and nobody but a native speaks Grakel; it sounds like a bunch of stones being rattled in a dish, all consonants and no vowels. It's difficult even for a priestess of Tor, and we're trained in languages from early childhood."

The Beak asked, "Is there a *lingua franca*?"

"A what?"

"A common tongue. A shared language."

"Well...travelers and traders, seamen and merchants speak Elsh—Parsnel—it's known as 'the tongue for trading and loving, the language for poets and thieves.' It's my native speech, I'd be pleased to teach it to you."

The Beak said, "It sounds fascinating."

Long Harry said, "It certainly fits us."

I said, "I've never been very good at learning languages."

"Don't worry about it," Long Harry said. "You're never very good at running until you're being chased." The incurable optimist.

"What do we do when we get away from here?" I asked, holding in reserve any doubts I might have about Long Harry's ability to perform the miracle he had so casually promised Thalla. I know when to keep my mouth shut.

"Judging by Thalla's sacred language, there are obviously Earthmen somewhere on the planet," The Beak said. "We'll have to figure out some way to get in touch with them."

"Why?" Long Harry asked.

The Beak looked the question over from several angles before answering. "You don't have to if you don't want to. I have unfinished business on Earth. I can find a way to get back from a, ah, homestead planet, but I can't get back from here without a transmatter. The thing we arrived here on isn't one of ours."

"My point," Long Harry said. "Consider this: any Earthmen here are here illegally. Look around you—this planet would obviously be interdicted right after contact. It has an intelligent native species at the pre-spaceflight level. Not only that, they're so humanoid as to probably be human. I have no idea of what the explanation for that is, but I'm damn sure that if this were an open planet we'd have heard of it."

Thalla was looking confused at all this, but she didn't ask any questions.

I did. "How can Earthmen be here illegally?"

"You have a naïve view of the universe," Long Harry told me. "Consider that any time there is a chance for a man to make a substantial profit, legally or il-, he will find a way. Here, I will weave you the tale:

"First there are the weave ships plowing through the universe at somewhere between two and three lights...."

"About two and a quarter," I said helpfully.

"Relative to what? Don't believe everything you see on Colonel Lumpneck, the show is designed for eight-year-olds."

"I went to college," I insisted.

"Good-oh. As I was saying, somewhere between two and three lights. Due to the relativity factor, which I'm sure Doctor Daniel here will be delighted to explain to you at some later time, this is multiplied by a factor of about four back on Earth. The end result is that every Earth year, we get about nine light-years further out into the galaxy, in an ever-increasing sphere. Blow the bugles for man's progress.

"Now the crews on the weave ships serve a three-year hitch, ship time, for which, when they transmatter back to Earth, they get about twelve years' pay. A good deal in anybody's league. Their job is to find new planets, set up transmatters on them, and go on. A follow-up crew comes through the transmatter and does the exploring and makes the decisions. Like if there's an intelligent, indigenous life-form, the planet is interdicted unless and until the natives achieve space-drive for themselves. There are eleven or twelve of these interdicted planets. What's going to be interesting is the day that we stumble across a race more advanced than us; I await that development with interest.

"Anyway, the interdicted planets, of which I'm sure this is one, are a fertile ground for the con-men, swindlers, the hungrier businessmen, and incipient kings or gods among us. That's why the planets are interdicted in the first place. Just think, a ready-made labor force, easily impressed and pressed upon."

"How would they get here?" The Beak asked. "The trans-matter points to closed planets are carefully controlled by the government."

"True," Long Harry admitted. "But all you need is one confederate either among the weave ship or the follow-up crews. What they would do is plant a second transmatter, tuned to a different key-set, and you have your own door to Eldorado."

"You think that's what happened here?" I asked.

"I do," Long Harry said. "And that's why I wonder whether we should chance getting in touch with the Earthmen here. Since they're criminals, they wouldn't dare return us to Earth; we might expose them. The best we could expect is closely-watched jobs here. I'm against it, at least until we have a lot more information."

"I see what you mean," The Beak said. "Still, I do want to get back to Earth somehow."

Long Harry shrugged. "If worse comes to itself, we can always hijack their station. We'll discuss it again later, when we know more. The job now is to get out of here."

"No argument," I said.

Thalla said, "I thought my understanding of this speech was good, but I didn't understand what you said, although I knew most of the words. You will have to explain."

"Well...." Long Harry was hesitant.

"What can they do to us?" The Beak asked. "Okay, child. Explanations are in order. The least we can do, if you're going to help us, is tell you what's going on. I hope you have an open mind." He sat down and started explaining about stars and planets. It turned out that she already knew about stars and planets. He told her there were people on other planets; she wasn't surprised. That simplified things, although it made me wonder exactly how primitive these people were.

While the lecture continued, Long Harry had me help him. We were making something that looked like a witch's broom, by tying lengths of the driest straw we could find to the end of the six-foot stick The Beak had found earlier.

"It'll never fly," I said, examining our handiwork. "And even if it does, we can't fit it through the bars."

"The purpose of this little artifact is to spread the bars so that we can fly, leaving it behind," Long Harry informed me.

"Oh." My immediate thought was that Long Harry had flipped, but I suppressed it. The only thing thinking like that would accomplish would be to depress me, and I was already sufficiently depressed.

"I will demonstrate later in the day, hopefully. Right now the thing to do is relax, take it easy. Do you play chess?"

"Yes, but not very well."

"Relax. Your muscles are tense. Do some sit-ups. Pawn to king four."

"I can't play without a board."

Long Harry looked at me as if I had just confessed congenital idiocy; but he forbore comment. Instead he took his own advice and did a quick twenty sit-ups. Then he rolled over and appeared to go immediately to sleep.

I did five sit-ups, three push-ups, and stared at the wall. A string of animals galumphed through the corridor, raising a cloud of straw dust that filled my throat and lungs. I coughed for a while. Then I gave that up and tried lying down on my back so I could stare at the ceiling for a change, but after a few seconds I sat up quickly when one of the lumps under me scurried into the next cell. The day wore on slowly.

Long Harry opened his eyes and sat up. "I judge it's time. Daniel, you help me. Beak, Thalla, stay back in the cell. If anything goes wrong, drop to the ground and cover your mouth and nose; there'll be a lot of smoke, but I doubt if any of this straw is dry enough to actually burn."

"Burn?" I stood. "You're going to. set the place on fire?"

"I hope not. I judge it to be about time for the evening gallop. My idea is to annoy the animals."

"Whatever you're talking about," The Beak said, "I hope it works. You have my best wishes for a successful conclusion."

"Mine is not to reason why...," I said.

Thalla broke in, "If you're planning to do something about or with the beasts, they are approaching now."

"I don't hear anything," I said.

"I'm sorry. Nonetheless, they thunder toward us."

Long Harry flattened himself against the bars and thrust the improvised broom through, probing toward the oil lamp set in the niche in the wall. "I can't see," he said. "Guide me, Daniel."

"Up. Now out more—you're about a foot short of it. That's the way. Another six inches...."

Long Harry groaned and stretched. "It's no use," he said. "That's as far as I can reach."

"Use Daniel as a support," The Beak suggested.

"Right. Come here Daniel, so I can step on you."

"Why me?"

Long Harry said, "I'll answer your philosophical questions later. Come here, there's no time."

I could now hear the pitter-patter of very large feet coming down the corridor, so I went over and knelt by the corner, bending over so Long Harry could climb on my back. He did, and balanced on one foot to reach the niche, grinding his heel into my back muscles.

"Ow!"

"Later, I think I've got it. Ah...there." There was a crashing sound. Long Harry stepped off my back. "That was the tricky part; getting the straw soaked with oil and lighting it without putting out the flame." He pulled the blazing broom tip carefully into the cell. "The rest is a snap. It might not work, but it's a snap."

He went to the other corner of the cell and stuck the broom out between those bars, inserting the burning end carefully into the straw matting of the cell across the corridor. The flame burned fitfully for a few seconds and then disappeared. "Shit!" Long Harry said. The thudding animals were much closer now.

Wisps of gray smoke curled up from the straw. A tongue of flame appeared. Then the corner went up, belching flame and billowing smoke. "Most satisfactory," Long Harry said.

"We're going to burn up," I announced. "That's no way to get out of here."

"It's one way," The Beak said. "We're not going to burn up. Have faith."

The beasts, six armor-plated specimens, came, single-file, into view. The smoke, pure white steam from the damp straw, rose to meet them. The first creature shied when it saw the fire, and tried to slow down. The beast behind rammed into it. It made a noise like a dying foghorn, and charged straight ahead. This panicked the ones behind, who could only see the smoke but not the fire, into single-file stampede.

The first beast raced by our cell and the fire without pause, and thundered down the corridor, raising a cloud of strawdust and smoke.

Then a sheet of flame, like an indoor lightning bolt, seared the room as the strawdust-air mixture caught fire. The hot air spread like the draft from a blast furnace, then ended. The second beast, maddened by fear, careened into the side of the next cell, bending the bars in like soft plastic, and bounced off the cell across the way before thundering after the leader. The ones behind were bouncing from side to side in the narrow corridor like pool balls after a bad break. By the time the last one had squealed and trumpeted its way out of sight, the cell bars fronting the corridor had been sprung and twisted out of shape like a piece of Yaji sculpture.

Then silence. The fire seemed to be out, although wisps of smoke still came up from widely scattered places around the cell-filled room. I took a deep breath and rubbed my hand along my arm, surprised to find that the hair hadn't been burnt off, I was whole and unhurt, although my eyes itched from the smoke.

"That's that," Long Harry said. "Come on, let's get out of here."

"This was your scheme?" I asked.

"Well, just about. I wasn't counting on the explosion, but it worked out very well."

"Very well," The Beak agreed. "Let's get out of here."

"We could have all been killed," I said.

"But we weren't," Long Harry said, twisting at the. bars.

"We're still alive," The Beak agreed. "Now let's get away from here."

We squeezed between a pair of battered bars without too much trouble and trotted down the corridor in the direction the animals had came from. Some of the other cells had prisoners in them, but they were too frightened or beaten to move and we decided not to encourage them.

The corridor turned into a poorly lit, stone tunnel, which twisted to the left and up. After a second turn, the tunnel opened into a large room, which held the empty cages the beasts had been released from. The room was empty of people. It had five wooden doors at the far end and a large double door, for admittance to the cages, to the right. All were closed.

"Take your pick," Long Harry said, indicating the doors with a sweep of his hand, "the lady, the tiger, the gorilla, the lawyer, or the bathroom; one of each, gift wrapped in five attractive colors."

"Spare me from the lawyer," The Beak said. "I'll take my chances with any of the others."

Long Harry shrugged. "We'll take them in order, from left to right. One of them's got to get us out of here." He went over to one of the cages, pulled off the bar used to secure the door, and hefted it in his hand. "Now I feel more secure," he said, going over to the first door. We were right behind him, and I think I held my breath while he pulled and twisted at the iron handle inset on the side of the thick wooden door.

"Argh!" Long Harry stepped back from the door, holding his iron bat like Casey. "It's either locked or barred."

"Well, don't swing at it, please," said The Beak. "Let's not have any unnecessary noise. Try the next one, perhaps it's open."

"You're right," Long Harry admitted. He approached the next door, grabbed the handle and swung it open. It led to a long hallway, and was guarded on the other side by a guard who seemed surprised to see us.

"Upish?" the guard said, turning around and grabbing for the pike leaning against the wall next to him.

Not even bothering with the iron bar, Long Harry drove a fist into the guard's chin. His head snapped back and he went. sprawling to the floor. We tiptoed cautiously into the hall, but there was no one else in sight.

The hall was filled with little iron-barred windows, all neatly shuttered from the inside. At the far end was a door. It was locked from our side, and opened onto the street.

CHAPTER SEVEN

A gust of clean air hit me in the face, and I realized how foul was the air I had been breathing for two days. The street was black and the sky overhead was filled with the glitter of unfamiliar stars.

"Where are we?" Long Harry asked. "Which way do we go?"

"The arena is just about in the center of the city," Thalla said. "The *Ta'P'Quisset* is by the *Ta'P'Flagget,* or old quarter."

"What's that?" I asked.

"The *Ta'P'Quisset* is the caravan-quarter. It's an independent section of the city, set aside for caravan drivers and other foreigners and non-citizens. They aren't allowed past the gates after dark."

"Will we have any trouble getting in?" Long Harry asked.

"I don't think so. Follow me. If anyone comes try to keep out of sight. Your clothing is strange enough to make people suspicious."

We crept single file through the darkened streets and alleys of Grak. Thalla seemed to have a sixth sense which warned her when people approached long before I could hear anything, and we'd huddle crouched in a doorway until they passed.

We entered an area where the streets fronted blank, high, windowless walls, some an entire block long, with one large door set into them.

"Rich nobles and merchants," Thalla explained in a whisper. "The houses are built around a central court and garden. Very private, very pretty. Hush! Hide, someone comes."

We dropped to the ground and flattened out against the wall. I tried to think like a stone.

Clop, throp-top, clop. Clop, throp-top, clop.

A carriage rounded the corner, pulled by something that looked like a short, fat, unicornidous camel. It approached, in no great hurry, the point where we lay.

Clop, throp-top, clop. Clop, throp.... It stopped. The beast swiveled its fat head around on its stubby neck and glared at us, one leg still raised to complete its lopsided gait, a study in frozen motion.

The driver of the carriage stood in place and started speaking in a steady monotone. It's interesting to note that one can recognize cursing even in a language one is completely unfamiliar with. The beast stayed frozen long enough to have posed for a life-size statue, while the driver's language got louder and more inflected. He dexterously applied a short whip to the animal's flanks, with a rhythmic slapping sound that had no effect on the beast. It kept, unblinkingly, staring at us, and we stayed flattened against the sidewalk.

The people inside the carriage finally got into the act. They seemed to blame the delay on the driver, and stuck their four heads out of the carriage window to yell at him. He gave up whipping the beast to swivel around and yell back at the passengers.

The passengers started waving fists and assorted objects at the driver, who shook his whip at them at the top of his voice. One of them produced a gold-knobbed cane from inside and started banging the roof with it. This was the final straw for the driver, who dismounted and went around to the carriage door. He thrust the whip in the passenger's face, and received, in reply, a thump on the top of his hat from the cane.

This discussion might have continued for some time, but the beast decided it was through staring at us.

Screwing its mouth sideways, it took a deep breath and spit directly at us. It hit me on the leg. Then it broke into a comfortable trot, leaving the driver standing, shaking his whip at the rear wheels. He yelled and ran after the animal, which speeded up its pace just enough so that he couldn't swing on board the carriage. They disappeared down the street like that; the driver hopping on one foot, trying to hook the other one onto the coach, the passengers, with their heads out the window, screaming at the animal and the beast keeping his speed just high enough to keep the driver hopping.

"I don't think I like that animal," I said when the entourage was out of earshot, wiping beast-spit off my trousers.

"You will grow even less fond," Thalla told me, giggling. "That's a pimpady—the animal you're going to be driving if I can get us jobs in a caravan. It was on good behavior, and they only pick the best-mannered ones to pull carriages."

We continued our stealthy journey toward the *Ta'P'Quisset* wall while I thought that over. It was another half hour before we reached the wall.

"What now?" Long Harry asked, staring up at the twenty feet of smooth stone. "I might be able to climb it, but not in the dark."

"It won't be necessary," Thalla said. "We'll just walk around the wall."

"I don't want to be picked up by any guards," Long Harry said.

"Don't worry, the guards don't leave the gatehouse at night, and we'll walk away from the gate." And so we did: in a group, boldly but quietly we walked down the middle of the street next to the wall.

"Sssst! Sssst!"

We stopped and looked around. Someone was beckoning to us from the top of the wall. Thalla answered him, and they had a brief conversation.

"What does he say?" I asked.

"He says he'll get us over the wall for six fegrak apiece. I offered him three, and we settled on fifteen for the lot."

"Great," I said. "Let's go."

"How are we planning to pay him?" asked The Beak. "I don't

know about you, but I don't have a fegrak to my name."

"I'll pay him," Thalla said. She ran her fingers through her hair and pulled out a loop of wire. "Gold hairpins are the Sisterhood's emergency traveling currency—it's an old trick."

A rope ladder cascaded down the wall and we climbed it one at a time, Long Harry first and The Beak last. The wall entrepreneur was a short, stocky man dressed in Early Egyptian. He pulled the rope up after us, took his wire pay, bit it, weighed it in his hand, grumbled a bit, and led us over the roof of a house built up against the wall to the street below.

We settled against some convenient straw in the courtyard to sleep until morning. I was getting very sick of sleeping on straw, but we had no money for an inn and they probably wouldn't open for us that time of the night anyway. Well, clean straw was better than filthy, damp straw, cool fresh air was better than dank, stinking air, and the star-filled sky was infinitely preferable to stone walls and ceilings. I lay on my back and stared at strange constellations until my eyes closed.

My last thoughts before I dozed off were that I had somehow become the junior member of this group, gopher boy and bottle washer; and it was about time I did something more to earn my keep and gain a little status in the eyes of my companions— particularly the female one, who was snuggled comfortably in the crook of The Beak's arm. After all, he was old enough to be her father. All night I dreamt heroic dreams.

Early the next morning we were bargaining with a pimpa- digrotgraf—caravan leader to you. Thalla did the talking for us, while we stood by looking smug. His point was that, while he was perfectly willing to use escaped slaves, we should be willing to work just for passage. Our point was that nobody but escaped slaves or criminals or madmen would sign on to go across the Great Marsh, so he needed us just as much as we needed him; after all, only one caravan in three made it across. If I had known at the time what our point was, I probably wouldn't have looked so smug.

After much talk a price was agreed, and everyone smiled and

rubbed thumbs: the traditional way of sealing a verbal agreement. Then the pimpadigrotgraf smiled even more broadly and added one more sentence before trotting away. Thalla's face fell.

"What is it?" I asked.

"We're leaving in an hour," she said.

The Beak asked, "What's wrong with that? The sooner we're away from here, the better."

"Yes, but that means he must be short on help to hire us so soon before starting out. I could have gotten a better price."

"We'll forgive you," Long Harry told her, patting her back. "You did very well."

The caravan was to be escorted for one day's ride out of Grak by a troop of local soldiers. We were to stay out of sight until they left. The usual place of concealment was the cook wagon, but six runaway apprentices had prior claim. We were given well-worn marsh garb, a sort of hooded sackcloth muumuu, and told to mix with the other drivers and pretend we knew what we were doing. It was all a formality anyway; right before the soldiers turned back the leader could demand to search the cook wagon and be given his usual bribe to forget it. Thalla was installed in the second wagon as the pimpadigrotgraf's concubine. This was, he assured us, only to keep her inconspicuous; his wife would kill him if he tried to take advantage of the situation. Once out of Grak she would revert to cook's helper.

The wagons formed and headed out the main gate. We fell in behind, part of a group leading the relief pimpadies. Each of us had four animals by the lead lines, which went through a ring set in the nose. our only problem was to keep them moving while staying out of reach of the recurve horns. Which is, in a sense, the only problem of a matador.

By the end of the first few hours I was thoroughly tired and bruised. The beast's horns had been filed down and capped, but they could still give you a nasty bump. I picked up a short stick from the side of the road, and, the next time I caught one of them lowering its head to bring its horn into action, I clouted it on the nose. After a few clouts, the beasts were better behaved;

not more subdued, just wary. I spotted one getting ready to spit and batted it sharply. It looked surprised and dribbled. The pimpadies and I reached a truce, but I was more tired and sore; they would outlast me easily. And this trip was to last a month.

About half a day out a pimpady and rider appeared to our rear, approaching quickly. It was a soldier, delivering a message to the captain of our escort troop. After reading the message roll the captain trotted over to the pimpadigrotgraf and barked an order at him. Our boss barked back, using his hands expressively, but the captain was adamant. The caravan was stopped, and the soldiers searched the wagons.

They unearthed the six youths in the cook wagon and a bald old man hiding in a water-barrel wagon that even the pimpadigrotgraf didn't know about. After spilling a barrel of flour and somehow loosing a bolt of cloth so that it rolled down a hill, unwinding as it went, the soldiers called it quits. Gathering their captives to their collective bosom, they galloped back toward the city. Not one of them had nosed among the smelly pimpady-pullers.

We stopped that evening just before the sun went down and formed into a loose square with the beasts inside. The long day's work had made Long Harry cheerful and The Beak angry. Me, I was tired. We sat there in our various attitudes discussing the day when Thalla came over with our supper and joined us. She handed us each an earthenware bowl full of steaming meat stew and a thick slice of bread and set down a large jug of greenwine. It smelled good. I suppose anything would have, and I sat there staring at it. I was too tired to eat. After a minute of breathing the fumes my hunger overcame my exhaustion and I dug in. There were no spoons, and the proper technique was to ladle the stew with the bread.

It was good. I cleaned the bowl until it didn't need washing and then gulped down the last morsel of gravy-soaked bread. The greenwine was good too. Its alcohol content was just high enough to inhibit the growth of germs, but it was tart, fruity, and filling.

The pimpadigrotgraf came over while we were eating and squatted on the hard ground, looking at us. He was a short, fleshy, worried-looking man, with a fringe of hair and lines of wrinkles forming inverted V's on his forehead. He talked to Thalla while we smiled pleasantly at him; then he went away, shaking his head.

The Beak sipped cautiously from the greenwine jug. "What does the old man want?"

"He doesn't like our table manners," Long Harry offered.

Thalla shook her head. "He came to tell me that the soldiers were looking for us."

"You mean us in particular?" I asked.

"That's right. The messenger brought word to look for three men who couldn't speak Grakel or Elsh and a Priestess of Tor who was in their company. We were to be brought back alive, if possible."

"Who'd take that sort of an interest in us?" The Beak asked.

"Our buddies from back home," Long Harry answered. "We're going to have to keep out of sight. Where's my bedroll?"

* * * * * * *

The next two weeks plodded along. We spent our time, when we weren't tending pimpadies or jacking up the sides of wagons to replace broken wheels or axles, learning to speak Elsh. It was a positional language with very precise words and several sounds not native to English. Mastering the new sounds was the hardest part. Thalla and The Beak worked to make vocabulary easy. Thalla was a competent empath; which meant that she was able to receive impressions, not actual thoughts, and the Beak was a trained hypnotist. He seemed to have had a variety of professions. Anyway, with their aid Conversational Elsh became almost fun. I would spend the days pulling recalcitrant pimpadies and reciting vocabulary to Long Harry or The Beak. We made up a set of Guidebook Phrases; Caravans, For use on. Like:

GOOD DAY (SIR) (MADAM) (PIMPADY), HOW ARE
    YOUR FEET?
THEY BOUNCE, THANK YOU. IT IS TOO MUCH.
HOW MANY FEGRAK COSTS THAT OBJECT?
I WILL GIVE YOU HALF THAT MUCH, BUT ONLY IF YOU
INCLUDE THAT WORTHLESS OBJECT THERE ALSO
PLEASE HELP ME, I AM A STRANGER HERE
      (LOOKING FOR A PLACE TO STAY)
      (BEING BITTEN BY SOMETHING SMALL AND
        BAD-TEMPERED)
      (SINKING IN QUICKSAND)
      (GOING TO THROW UP)
I NEED A DOCTOR
      (A POLICEMAN)
      (A REST)
      (A JOB)
      (A DRINK)
YOUR WAGON IS VERY PRETTY
      (HEAVILY LOADED)
      (STUCK IN THE MUD)
      (RESTING ON MY FOOT)
THIS ANIMAL HAS A GLOSSY COAT
      (A MEAN DISPOSITION)
      (A SECRET PLAN)
      (GREEN DROOL)
      (JUST EATEN MY HAT)
YOU ARE MOST KIND
      (IN IMMEDIATE DANGER OF BEING SPAT ON)
      (BLEEDING)
      (GOING TO HIT ME)

There are a lot of colorful phrases in Elsh that relate to the
handling of pimpadies, but as they mostly relate to anatomy,
biology and genealogy, three technical subjects, I won't bore
you with them here.

By the end of the first week we had left the territory of Grak and entered the Great Marsh. Picture a fresh water mud pie about the size of France, crusted with lush green and purple vegetation, brightly flowered and heavily thorned, trapped, and poisoned, laced with ridges of bare rock that had a well-developed knack for turning into quicksand; and alive with a weird variety of unfriendly animals, from little squirrel-like pests that attacked with insane fury anything that moved, to marsh lions that consider humans as a pleasant change in diet. That's the first impression of the Great Marsh; after you get to know it, it doesn't seem nearly as nice as that.

We kept to the ridges of flat, gray rock as much as possible. It was a well-traveled route. Three or four times a day we'd pass the wreck of a caravan wagon sinking into the mud and being pulled apart by creepers.

The work was hard, boring and dangerous. The hours were long and the weather was lousy. I decided not to reenlist.

The other drivers, now that we could understand them, delighted in telling us horror stories of previous caravans they had been on. I discounted ninety percent of what they said as outrageous exaggeration, and was still scared. There was the *Kibu*, a sort of parrot-roc that would fly low over a caravan asking questions, and occasionally pick up a pimpady or a driver and fly off to do the gods know what with him. There were the *uggats*, giant hippo-like herbivores that grazed in groups of several hundred and would stampede at the slightest insult, flattening everything and everyone in their path. There was the bouncer, a plant that, at one point in its life cycle, would start thumping the ground, building up to a paradiddle crescendo, and then explode, blasting its seed pods high into the air and destroying everything within a fifty-yard radius.

These were mere annoyances. The real dangers, as on any planet, came from the people. There were Marsh Rogues in great variety, nasty hermits or families who lived hidden in the marsh and would haunt a caravan, stealing goods and picking up stray pimpadies or people. They probably enslaved the people, although there were stories of rogue cannibalism. Then there were the pirates—several tribes of raiders that lived in secret clear areas in the marsh and supported themselves by attacking caravans. There were many wild stories about them, including one group which supposedly had flying ships. They captured and enslaved caravaniers for resale, ransom, or home use.

About two weeks into the marsh a lizard wrapped itself around my leg and tried to chew it off. I grabbed a stick and swatted it, knocking it loose, and then flattened it. It was still chewing when it died. About three hours later I came down with a fever. Thalla unbound the chew marks in my leg to check for signs of infection, and spotted a small scratch above the wound. I had pricked myself slightly with a thorn in the stick.

"You should have told me right away," Thalla said severely, cutting the scratch open with her belt knife.

"I'm sorry. I didn't notice it at the time. I was busy."

"I think I can save you," Thalla said.

"Save me?" People shouldn't try to frighten you when you're sick.

Thalla misunderstood my tone. "I know I'm only a girl," she said, "but I've been trained for the sisterhood for years. Many of the sisters are mistresses in the doctor's guild, and I'm ready to take the journeyman's examination as soon as I come of age. Beak says I'm very competent. He says I have the healing touch and that, combined with my empathy sense, it could make me a great doctor."

"The Beak says?"

"Well, he's a doctor himself. He should know."

"Of course." Nobody ever tells me anything.

"This will hurt."

"Ow."

"Hold still."

"OW!"

"There, the tip of the thorn. We got it before it went in too deep. And you're bleeding freely now, that'll wash the remaining gunk out. I'll suck the cut for a minute just to make sure." She bent down and put her lips to the fresh X she had just cut in my leg.

"Isn't that dangerous?" I asked. "I mean, if there's any poison left...."

She spat to the side. "Not unless I swallow it. Probably not even then, but why take chances?" She sucked and spat a few more times, then wrapped my multiple wound in fresh bandage cloth. "You're going to have a high fever for a few days, but you won't burn up; I caught it just in time. You shouldn't walk, in fact you probably won't be able to. I'll get the pimpadigrotgraf to put you in a stretcher in my wagon."

And I wasn't. And she did. And he did. The next morning I was riding along in a hammock slung inside the cook wagon. I was unconscious and, if not exactly delirious, at least having some very bad dreams. I cried a lot and screamed a bit and Thalla sat beside me and kept me mopped down with cold, moist cloths.

Just as Thalla had predicted, I came out of my fever and my reverie two days later. The Beak was leaning over me, swaying from side to side, when I opened my eyes. No—I was swaying from side to side, or, more accurately, my hammock was. The wagon, with its wheels removed, was fording a swamp and rocking to the time of the polemen who were pushing it through the weed-covered sludge.

"Hello," I said, focusing on The Beak's face.

"The least you can do is be traditional," be said crossly. "'Where am I?' is your line. How do you feel?"

"Dizzy." Everything looked blue and out of line.

"I can't say I'm surprised. That's a very potent drug that plant's carrying around."

"I think I'll go back to sleep now," I said. "It's been nice talking to you."

When I woke up again, I was alone in the wagon. My hammock was swinging from side to side with a ponderous rhythm. The polemen outside were pushing in time to an Elsh chant and I was staring at the roof and hallucinating. The words from the chant appeared on the whitewashed wagon ceiling in

Gothic shapes and pastel colors. They lined up in ranks and rows and rearranged themselves into English. The original, being round-robined outside, was a traditional marsh chanty. My ceiling was peremptorily revising it into a warped *Little Willy*. I think I argued for some time with the ceiling, but it insisted on its version.

> *Willy was the hero type:*
> *Brave Willy.*
> *He drew his sword and blew his pipe,*
> *And faced the foe without a gripe*
> *And slew the tyrant who thought he might*
> *Enslave Willy.*

> *(Gripe? Might?* Oh well....*)*

> *Willy fought the dread Blue Bear*
> *For fun Willy.*
> *He fought it hard, he fought it fair,*
> *He fought it long outside its lair;*
> *He killed it then and left it there.*
> *Well done, Willy.*

> *Willy bragged about his kill,*
> *Did Willy.*
> *He wrote long odes about his skill*
> *And read aloud, as poets will.*
> *His rhymes were poor, but all kept still;*
> *Kid Willy?*

> *Now all will sing the poetry*
> *Of Willy.*
> *Heroic tales from sea to sea:*
> *How one man fought to keep all free!*

Our meter's bad, but that shows we
Love Willy.

The punctuation kept jumping around. There was more, but it ran into the overhang and was too dark to read.

There was a series of thumps from outside and the singing stopped. The wagon tilted onto its side and stayed there for a minute. Then the front end was lifted high into the air, to the company of much shouting and cursing, and shortly the rear end joined it. Then a series of jerks and we were rolling again.

Thalla came in with some strong bark tea and a cup of gruel. "We're back on wheels," she said. "Are you awake enough to eat?"

"I think I can even manage to feed myself," I told her, struggling to get out of the hammock. I tried to sit up, but the hammock just adjusted to my shape and held me more firmly. Finally I rolled over and fell out. "There," I said firmly, lying on my stomach. "Now, if the floor will just hold still...." I pushed myself up to a sitting position and crossed my legs. "I'm weak."

"Naturally," She handed me the gruel. "If you eat, you'll get strong. Come on, now, eat this all up."

"Why is it," I appealed, waving my cup of tea at the roof, "that nurses always treat their patients like small children? At least you didn't say, 'let's take our bath now.'"

"Bathing," Thalla told me severely, "is always done in private."

"Sharing a tub can have its good points," I informed her. "I'll have to discuss it with you sometime." I tasted the gruel.

CHAPTER EIGHT

"ATTACK! ATTACK!
"GATHER HERE!
"UP SWORDS!
"STAKE THE BEASTS!
"ATTACK!"
"ATTACK!"

Something was happening outside the wagon. It jerked violently from side to side, then swayed forward, picking up speed in two-foot bounces.

"What the...," I said, trying to hang onto my cup and bowl. Hot tea sloshed all over my arm.

"We're being attacked," Thalla said calmly, drawing herself into as small a ball as possible and looking scared.

"I figured that," I yelled, losing my grip on the bowl, which made it across the room on one bounce and splattered against the door, "but by what?"

The wagon suddenly hit molasses and pulled to a stop, sending us head over heels against the forward wall. It teetered delicately for a moment, ass end up, and then crashed over on its side. The left side paneling—which was now the roof—sagged inward, cracked, splintered and fell all around us. A large water barrel, which had been strapped to the outside, crashed next to me, cascading us with water and staves.

The sky was full of ships. Viking ships they looked like, lean, wooden superstructures with a row of basket shields along the sides and garishly-painted monster figureheads. The masts were missing, replaced by long lines that went up to a pair of huge gasbags. Small sails were affixed to the lines.

Ropes had been dropped over the sides of the ships, which were about forty feet from the ground, and men were sliding down, gleaming, curved swords in their mouths, protected by archers at the gunnels. I couldn't see the ground near the wagon, but the sound of sword fighting—or of a group of men hammering on iron boxes—was coming from all around.

"Are you all right?" I asked Thalla. There was no answer. "Are you all right?" I insisted, pulling myself out of the wreckage and searching for her. She was lying quite still under a wooden side brace, her face covered with blood.

I couldn't move the brace, so I worked myself around to her side and pulled her loose as best I could. I felt for a pulse and couldn't find any, which frightened me; but I had no idea if I was doing it right or not. I put my ear to her face and convinced myself that I could hear breathing.

The clanking and screaming were getting louder, and the ships seemed to be closer to the ground. I looked around and spotted what seemed to be the door to a large, iron box ahead of me. I was afraid to pull Thalla any further, so I took the chance of standing up and lifted her in my arms. This business of "light as a feather" sounds okay when you read it, but a hundred and ten pounds is a hundred and ten pounds, and I was very weak to start with. I staggered over to the box, tripping on some debris and almost dropping her, and sank down beside it.

I must have lost consciousness, because the next thing I knew there was a great pounding sound coming from outside the wagon. I struggled with the handle until I could twist it open. The door was heavy cast iron, and opened because of the way the box had fallen. A small cloud of soot hit me in the face. Coughing and sputtering, I stuck my head in and inspected the box. It was quite roomy inside, dropping down below the level of the door for about four feet—it must have turned on its side and gone right through the wall of the wagon, burying itself partly in the marsh below—and empty except for a few ashes.

I managed to prop the door up with a small, broken barrel, and pulled and pushed Thalla through the opening, lowering her as gently as I could to the floor. I had intended to find another hiding place for myself, but this was easily big enough for two, so I crawled in after her and pushed the barrel aside with a stick. The door slammed down with a loud clank, which I could only hope no one had heard, and I settled myself down on the bed of ashes.

This time I didn't lose consciousness, I just lost interest. I was too weak to move and too tired to care. If someone had swung the door open and stuck a sword in my face, I wouldn't even have smiled at him.

The fighting noises got louder for a while, then they stopped. After a while a new noise started, a curious crackling and snapping. I lay there trying to figure out what it was but I couldn't gather enough energy to stand up and open the door.

The noise died down and I fell asleep. I didn't dream. When I woke up something was poking me in the stomach. "Argh!" I said.

"Daniel? Is that you?" Thalla asked. It was, I discovered, her foot poking me.

"It's me," I told her. "Could you move your foot?"

She did. "What happened? I don't remember."

"We got attacked," I told her. "And the side of the wagon fell in on you. Balloonships, very strange looking. How are you feeling?"

"I think I'm blind," Thalla said.

"How could you tell?" I asked. "There's no light in here."

"Oh. Well, that explains it then. Where are we?"

"We're hiding in some kind of iron box."

"Iron box? Do you think it's safe to go out now?"

"I don't know. I fell asleep myself. I guess the only thing to do is take a look." I stood up and cautiously lifted the door enough to peer out through the bottom. "It must be night, all I can see is black. Oh, no; there's just something in the way, I'll see if I can move it. Ouch!"

"What's the matter," Thalla whispered.

"I just burned my hand." I poked more carefully and succeeded in clearing some of the debris away. "Well, now I understand. The wagon's been burnt. The wood's just about cold but the metal isn't. The outside of this box is, ah, quite warm to the touch." I raised the lid up higher. "It's not night, just early afternoon. I'll see if I can get out. There doesn't seem to be anyone around."

I unbuttoned the hood of my robe and used it to insulate my hands while I boosted myself up and rolled forward, out of the box. Then I propped up the door and stuck my head back inside.

"Give me your hand, let me help you out of there."

When she was out I stood up to inspect the wreckage. "The balloonships seem to be gone," I said. "The only thing in sight in the sky is that bird way up there. I'll see if I can find some water. We both need to clean up. Your face is covered with blood."

She put her hands up to her face and inspected. "It's sticky all over, but I don't seem to be cut anywhere. I must have gotten a nosebleed."

"The water casks are all busted and mostly burnt. This section of the wagon isn't too badly burnt though. There might be something here. Aha! Here's a skin, and it seems partly full." I lifted it over my head and let some of the cool liquid stream over me. It stung when it reached my bruised forehead. I stopped pouring and tasted it as it dribbled off my nose. "Green-wine," I said. "Both good to drink and antiseptic; the best of all possible worlds. Here, take it and drink some, then clean off your face."

"Very good, my lord," Thalla said, attempting a curtsy.

"The fire must have been the strange noise I heard. I wonder why the inside of the box stayed cool."

"Insulation works both ways," Thalla said. "That box is the baking oven."

"Ah! Now why didn't I think of that."

"You don't do much baking?" Thalla offered kindly.

WHAP!

THUNG!

Thalla and I were each encased in the giant claws of a bird, which was regaining altitude with no apparent trouble. The bird I had noticed before had gone into a power dive, come to a dead stop six feet over our heads, grabbed us, one to each claw, and was off. I was being held firmly enough that I had a little trouble taking deep breaths, but I wasn't hurt.

I was, however, surprised, shocked, stunned, and quite speechless. I would like to go into a detailed description of the size, shape, coloration and plumage of my captor, but I had no better idea than a mouse does of a falcon. It was certainly the largest bird I had ever seen, by several orders of magnitude. Its underpinnings, which stretched quite a way in most directions, were blue. The wings were about the size of an intercity passenger plane and were black, at least on the bottom.

Thalla had started kicking and screaming when we were grabbed but I had been too shocked for that. She must have mistaken my shock for courage, because after a minute she stopped struggling and looked at me. "Can you make it let us go?"

"I, ah, don't think that would be too wise," I said. "We must be a couple of hundred feet up." I had looked down a few seconds before, and was now clutching the talon at least as hard as it was clutching me.

Thalla looked down and started screaming again. High, ear-piercing screams that didn't stop. I didn't blame her, and there was absolutely nothing I could think of to do.

A great bird's head, about three times the size of my body, with a long, skinny beak, undercurved at the end, appeared upside down in front of us. "Listen, food," it said in a high-pitched voice, "could you please stop screaming? It makes me nervous, and I'm liable to drop you."

To even my own surprise, I didn't say "Hey, a talking bird!" What I said was, "If you'll put us down somewhere, Oh Bird, I can get her to stop screaming."

The bird considered this for a minute. "You're trying to trick me," it said finally, and returned to looking where it was going.

Thalla stopped screaming and stared at me. "Did that bird really talk?" she asked in a calm voice, with just the slightest undertone of terror.

"I heard it too," I assured her.

The bird ducked its head down for a second, said "Thank you," and lifted.

"The Kibu!" Thalla said.

"What?" I tried to get into a more comfortable position. This was worse than third class.

"The mythical Kibu. The talking bird. I thought it was just a tale."

"It seems to be mostly wing," I told her, but she didn't notice. I shifted around again. "If you know what it is, there's nothing to worry about." Name magic, but maybe it would cheer her up. What good cheering up Thalla would do, I didn't know.

"The Kibu that abducts travelers, who are never again seen by man." she said.

There was something to worry about.

"I remember a caravan only a few years ago that claimed a rich merchant had been captured by a Kibu." Thalla said. "They arrested everybody, thinking it was a cover-up story. I guess it was true. Too bad; everyone in the caravan was executed."

"Too bad," I agreed, squirming.

The Kibu's head appeared upside down again. "Listen food, if you don't stop wiggling, I'll drop you."

"Is that your only threat?" I snarled. "And why do you keep calling us 'food'?"

"So that you know your place," it said. "What do you call your food?"

"Irving," I said.

"I'll call you that, if it'll make you feel better."

"Never mind."

The journey continued. The great bird's wings flapped slowly and ponderously, as the ground sped past hundreds of feet below. I wondered what it was about this planet that would allow a bird to grow to this size, when Earth's largest birds were far smaller, even the ones that had given up flight in favor of size. There was something called square-cube law, but I couldn't remember how it went. Anyhow I wasn't about to tell the Kibu that there was a law against it, it would only have gotten angry. I seemed to remember that the flying dinosaurs had gotten pretty big, but this thing was larger.

The head appeared again. "Look below," it said. "Over that way." It pointed with its beak.

Below and to the left were three of the gasbag ships. We were so far above them that they seemed to be skimming the ground. A volley of arrows suddenly arced out from the ships, their iron tips flashing in the rays of a sun which was low in the sky to our right. "They've seen us," I said foolishly, as the arrows fell far below us.

"They don't seem to like you," Thalla said to the Kibu.

"No," it said sadly. "Banquet always tried to hurt me."

"Banquet?"

"Yes," the bird said. "If you pierce those two round things, the creature falls, and there are a lot of beings like you inside that make good eating if you shell them properly. You don't have shells."

A very pragmatic bird.

"Why didn't you kill us first, then," Thalla asked. "We'd be easier to carry." I shot her a very dirty look, but the damage was done.

"I'm taking you home for my chicks," the bird told us. "You keep longer alive, and besides, the little darlings need the practice. You have to start them on harmless food first."

Harmless huh? The whole Human Race had just been insulted, but I didn't see what I could do about it. I decided to try guile, always a good surprise weapon. Ulysses had used it to great advantage, I remembered. At the moment, my supply of guile seemed very low. I decided to keep the creature talking, and maybe something would occur to me.

"How did you learn to talk?" I asked.

"My momma taught me," the bird said.

"I mean Elsh," I said. "How did you learn to talk Elsh?"

"From food like you. Do I talk well?"

"Very well. Exceeding well. You are a smart bird."

"I come from a smart hatching. Tell me a riddle."

"A riddle?"

"Don't you know any? I'll tell you one. I once kept a food around for many extra days because it taught me many riddles. It finally died anyway because I didn't know what to feed it. How many things do you have if you have two things and someone gives you two more things?"

"Four."

"Four what?"

"Four, ah, things."

"You've heard it before!" she said accusingly. I assume it was a she.

"I'm afraid your level of riddles is above me," I said. "Do you know any poetry?"

"What's that?" she asked suspiciously.

"That's a way of putting groups of words together so they have rhyme and meter."

"What are rhyme and meter?"

"Rhyme is when the sounds at the end of each group of words are the same, and meter is the, ah, bounce of the words."

"What's the good of it?"

"It makes a pleasing noise."

"Make one."

"Right." I stopped to think. Better keep it simple. I translated a classic pattern from English.

"Roses are red" I said, enunciating carefully.

"Violets are blue,

"We fly through the air

"Like a portable zoo."

(I had actually used two rather obnoxious marsh plants, and described their odor rather than their color.)

"It does bounce," the bird said, "Make another."

"Let me choose my rhymes," I said. "Ah:

"Roses are red,
"Violets are blue,
"From up here you get
"A remarkable view."

"I hope she's not a critic, or we're sunk," Thalla murmured at me.

"Does a poetry always start the same?" the bird asked, peering closely at me. She had bad breath.

"Each bit of poetry is called a poem," I told her. "This is just one pattern; there are many others."

"I will make one," the bird decided. She withdrew her head.

"What good does this do?" Thalla asked.

"The idea," I replied, "is to keep her interested."

"So we can starve to death?"

"Where there's life, there's hope," I told her. "So the idea is to keep the former going as long as possible."

"I never learned to think that way," Thalla said. "But you are right. I had given up hope back in the arena, and then again in the dungeon, and you got us out."

"Well, actually I didn't do much."

"That's true, but you helped."

"Thanks."

"Roses are red," the bird announced, sticking her head back at us,

"Violets are blue,

"Tomorrow morning

"I'm going to eat you."

"You have a one-track mind," I said.

"Was it a poetry?"

"A poem. Yes, it was a poem. But you're supposed to use a little imagination; keep it more impersonal."

"Oh," she said. She returned her head to upright.

The wings beat a slightly syncopated rhythm as she thought. Then they straightened out, and we went into a long glide. The great head peered under at us, and there was a glint in her eye. She recited:

"Roses are red,
"Violets are blue.
"There are my chicks,
"They'll eat you too."

"There are many other forms of poetry," I said hastily. "Perhaps you'd prefer one of those."

"Hold on," she said. She dove, and then stopped short six feet above her target with a mighty flapping of wings, and released us. We dropped to the ground and tumbled, and she settled lightly a few feet away.

We were on a rock ledge about a hundred feet above the ground. On one side the sheer wall of a cliff dropped straight into the marsh below, and on the other it scooped out an unclimbable overhang and then rose out of sight. The sun, just balanced on top of a distant mountain, cast dark shadows, and a hazy red light barely illuminated the sides of the shallow cavern which undercut the cliff like a giant ear in the side of the mountain.

On the far side of the great bird a few score massive tree trunks had been intertwined into a gigantic nest. When Momma had landed, a great chirping had started inside the nest, and the structure trembled with a loud rumbling sound.

"The little dears missed me," Momma said, sticking her head over the fifteen-foot side of the nest. "Hello, my little loves."

CHIRP
KREE
CHIRP
CHURP
KREE
CHURP

Momma tilted her head sideways at us and regarded us with one eight-inch, red eye. "The little loves are hungry."

"Would you, ah, like to hear a ballad?" I asked.

"Don't try to climb down the side," she said. "You'll fall and break. I'll be right back. I'm going to see if I can catch that banquet." With one flap of her great wings, she was off, and I was sitting on rock, knocked over by the blast.

"Well, what now?" Thalla asked, showing her great confidence in me. I wished I were nearly that confident myself.

KREE?

A much smaller monster's head, about half the size of my body, peered over the log barricade and stared balefully at us. It was soon joined by two more. After the initial sound they just stared silently, beaks half open. An excited rustling noise kept up behind them, and occasionally a fourth head would hop into view, beak clicking, and drop behind again. The runt of the hatch, I decided. Cute little tyke.

"Now be good," I said, shaking a finger at them. "Momma wouldn't want you to play with your food."

"That's not funny," Thalla gasped.

"I'm sorry," I told her. "Gallows humor, and a feeble attempt."

There was a creaking sound behind me, and the hatchlings shifted their gaze. Their beaks snapped closed, and they excitedly started trying to climb out of the nest. Although the noise of timber cracking was impressive, the chicks themselves didn't make a sound; either instinct or good nest discipline.

Backing up against a far wall, with Thalla behind me for whatever little protection I could offer, I risked a glance over my shoulder. One of the balloon ships was hovering over the edge of the ledge, and a horde of men were descending the dangling ropes.

The birds burst free of their nest and barged out toward dinner. The men who were low enough dropped free of the ropes, knelt, and notched arrows in their short, recurve bows. One man, the first to land, stood in front of them, gauging the distance as the furious chicks approached. The smallest of the four hatchlings, the one which had kept hopping up to see us, was about three times the size of a man. The largest, about twice that.

The first chick raced toward the standing man. When it had

just about reached him, he yelled "Fire!" and plunged his sword deep into the thin neck poised above him.

Man and bird went down in a fury of blood and wings, and the other chicks kept coming. The men kept up the barrage of arrows until the birds had reached them, and then they grabbed for swords and started hacking. The birds hacked back with beak and claw. Feathers and men flew in every direction, The rest of the men dropped to the cliff as soon as they were low enough, and joined in the carnage. One by one, the birds dropped, until all four were lying lifeless on the rock. Almost three times as many men had fallen, and the cliff floor was littered with dead and wounded.

The leader, who was bleeding from deep slashes along the side of his face, blew a whistle to regroup his men, and stood looking over the scene. The last rays of the setting sun cast a blood-red glow over all.

"Retrieve as many arrows as you can," he shouted, "and get slings down here for the corpses and wounded. We don't want to leave anything for Kibu, and I'm not going to try and fight her in the dark."

"We'll be back!" one of the men shouted,

The leader scowled. "She'll be gone by then, but—yes, we'll be back."

The men cheered.

"Ah, Captain!" I called.

He turned to stare at us as we came forward. "Thank you for rescuing us," I said. "We were almost in serious trouble."

The leader kept staring at us, deep in thought. Then he shouted, "Tie these two up, we'll take them back with us."

CHAPTER NINE

The pirate's lair was a rectangular patch of high ground over half a mile long and a couple of hundred yards wide at the narrowest. The surrounding marsh made its presence known by a pervasive odor and an occasional infiltrated patch of bog. The rest of the pimpadigrot personnel were already there when they took us in. Very few of them had been injured in the battle, and only three had been killed. The reason, I found out, was that we had been taken almost completely by surprise. The lad who had been sent to the roof of one of the wagons to keep watch from attack from the sky was new to caravan life. He thought the balloonmen were a myth and his guard job a practical joke—like sending him out for a jar of trail grease or a left-handed pimpady whip—so he'd gone to sleep. The rest of the men would have ganged up on him if the pimpadigrotgraf hadn't stopped them, but I thought it was probably lucky. If they'd tried fighting back seriously against that crew, most of them wouldn't have stayed alive long enough to be taken prisoner.

When the ship arrived back at the camp it was pitch dark; they guided themselves in by means of a row of greasy flares placed in a triangular pattern on the ground. Thalla and I were immediately tossed into the prisoner compound, where we rolled up in a shared blanket and lay down. Thalla went to sleep within a few minutes, but I was awake much of the night; bothered equally by this new problem and by thoughts of the slender, warm body pressed close against my shoulder. I came to no conclusions.

The next morning Long Harry and The Beak found us sleeping together and gently shook us awake. "A pretty picture," The Beak grumbled, "romance in a prison camp."

"We were worried about you," Long Harry said, squatting by my shoulder. "What happened?"

I disentangled myself from the blanket and sat up. We shook hands all around; for some reason it seemed the thing to do. Thalla folded the blanket up into a small square and put it beside her. "It is very good that you're all, right," she said. "I have the utmost confidence in you. How do we get out of here?"

"Come on, Thalla," I said, rubbing my arms to get the blood circulating. "Give the man a chance; he hasn't been here much longer than we have."

Long Harry rubbed the tip of his nose. "As a matter of fact, I have a plan. It'll take some time, though. The important thing is for us all to stay alive and healthy long enough to put the plan into operation. I have no idea, as of yet, what our captors' plans for us are."

"I knew you'd think of something," Thalla said. "What do we do?"

"The first step is to gain the confidence of our fellow prisoners, or slaves, or whatever we are; make friends with them. That's enough for the time being. Now, what happened to you?"

"Well...." I told him about the talking bird, figuring that if he'd believe that, I'd believe he had a plan.

"Fascinating," he said when I finished.

"Incredible," The Beak added.

"Fearfully horrifying," Thalla said. "Daniel was very brave."

"Of course he was," Long Harry said, patting me on the back. "Of course he was."

The Beak looked at us in a fatherly manner. "You were both very brave. 'Tis truly an incredible story. Full of poetry. *'Roses are red, violets are blue'*...full of poetry."

"Well, what should I have done," I demanded, "recite Browning?"

"Now, there's an idea," The Beak said thoughtfully. "If you'd spouted from *The Ring and the Book* at her, she'd have been so confused she'd have dropped you."

The other prisoners were awake now, and wandering around in small, sullen groups. Our compound was made up of three rows of six structures that looked like large, two-handled umbrellas. Two posts came out of the ground. to a height of about ten feet. At the eight foot mark a circle of thin branches were tied and dowelled to the posts, then spread out and up to the ten-foot tent-canvas ceiling. There were no walls. These parasol-tents were a bit chilly but they kept off the rain. The whole was surrounded by a deep moat, half full of muddy water, and, on the far side of the moat, a high wooden palisade. The ground was all hard-stamped brown dirt, with nothing growing save a fringe of moss around the moat. The whole created an impression of Spartan simplicity, rather than prison drudgery. It was still very depressing.

A gong sounded two deep, important notes, and a section of palisade lowered to become a bridge over the moat. Three pirates strode across into the compound. They were dressed in dark leather leggings, tucked into leather knee boots, with leather pullover jackets, leather belts and leather suspenders that crossed on their chests. Two of them had red threads worked ornately into the cross-straps, but aside from that the uniforms were identical.

"Ho there, fellows," the one in the middle bellowed. "Come all of you, gather round me and sit down; I must speak with you." Either the man was completely fearless, or it just never occurred to him that some of us might bear a grudge.

We gathered around and sat down meekly enough; I could see that most of the men were still very confused and disorganized.

The speaker surveyed us all slowly. He was lightly bearded, with long brown hair, tied in back with a scrap of leather. Tucked under his left arm was a large, silver-capped scroll. "Is your grotgraf still alive or, if not, who is left in charge?"

The pimpadigrotgraf stood slowly up. "I am still alive," he

said blandly.

"Good. I will read to you the latest entry in the Lesser Scroll." He uncapped the scroll and unrolled it to the right section. Then in a clear voice he read a technical account of the attack and destruction of the caravan. He covered the actual fighting in a few concise sentences, then got down to the nitty gritty. "Twenty-three persons were taken alive, and the following in goods, wares, salvage, equipment and personal effects were sequestered:

forty bolts fabric, for wearing apparel
sixteen bolts material, tent grade
sixty-two assorted barrels and boxes containing tepau root and
    other commercial-grade herbs and spices
fourteen demijohn jugs essential oils, gums and resins
six jugs, lamp oil
nine barrels, flour
four barrels, pickled brownfish
eleven barrels, greenwine
two barrels, tar
one demibarrel, nails
eleven chests, personal effects
thirty-six swords
six cuts, *sheempja*
four needles
various pots, pans, jars, jugs, knives, spoons and other cooking
    apparatus."

He looked up from his reading. "Does that seem right to you, grotgraf?"

The pimpadigrotgraf shrugged. "I suppose. I didn't know about the sheempja, it is against our law to use the drug, but everything else was on our manifest."

"Excellent. Then, would you sign this please?" He produced a quill and covered inkwell from the cylinder around which the scroll was wrapped, opened the inkwell, dipped the quill and extended it. The pimpadigrotgraf shrugged again, stepped forward and, taking the quill, signed the document in the space.

"You realize that this doesn't make it any the less an act of piracy?" he asked, handing the quill back.

"Of course. I shall carefully avoid your magistrates. Now, I would like you all to step forward, one at a time, and give me your names, occupations, home addresses, and the approximate amount you can be ransomed for. Your status while in the camp will depend on the amount you are good for matched against our estimated collection costs. If the amount is less than twenty figrels in gold, just list yourself as a slave. I should warn you that if the amount you name is not collectable, things will go hard for you."

As the men got up and went forward to have their names entered in the Lesser Scroll, we held a quick conference. It was agreed that Thalla would tell the truth, as her position as a Priestess of the Second Order of Tor the Mighty might in some way protect her, besides sending a request to the Order for ransom. We, on the other hand, were going to prevaricate. Thalla told us that our accents might pass us as Southlanders, so Southlanders we were. Any attempt at truth would only confuse the issue.

So we stood in line, identified ourselves, and got enscrolled. When we left the keeper of the Lesser Scroll, we were forwarded to another line, where his two companions were collecting our clothing and giving out slave garb. This was an all-purpose canvas sack, without arms, that came down to about the knees and was belted at the waist. Thalla, who was in front of me, balked at this.

"I won't," she said, planting her feet and putting her hands on her hips.

"What's that?" one of them said. "Come on, lad, don't be shy. We have no time for that sort of thing. Take your clothes off. We have to search you, you know. It's nothing personal."

"I'm not a lad, I'm a girl, and a priestess of the Second Order of Tor the Mighty!"

"You're a what?" He took a close look at her. "By the Sacred Bubbles, so you are. Frap, why didn't you say something? This one's a girl."

The scroll keeper didn't even look up. "What should I have said? You should be able to tell the one from the other without my help."

"You're right, you're right, so I should. It's not a problem I usually have, but this one's so grubby. Timro, take her over to the women to be searched and garbed. Girl, go along with him."

The Beak, who was behind me in line, rubbed a finger along his nose. "'Tis very interesting, that."

"I'll play your game this time," I told him. "What's very interesting?"

"Doesn't it strike you as a bit unusual? Here we're prisoners—slaves—and they're treating Thalla with respect, or, at least, consideration, because she's a girl. No rape, no suggestive remarks, not even a snigger."

"That's true," Long Harry said. "It ain't like the old army."

"Maybe they've got a high moral standard," I suggested.

"Ha!" Long Harry snorted. "Not bloody likely."

"Then what do you suggest?"

"I think me," The Beak said, "that yonder pirate's nest is a matriarchy."

We went through the processing then, not having Thalla's excuse for avoiding it; shedding clothes, being searched and pulling itchy canvas sacks over our heads.

"How," I asked The Beak when we were safely out of hearing range of our clothier, "will this information help us?" I asked in Elsh. We had agreed that it would be better to be caught saying nasty things about our captors than speaking a language they couldn't understand. We had no idea how paranoid they might be.

The Beak shrugged. "I don't know that it will help us at all, except in so far as every bit of knowledge acquired increases our understanding of the Universe."

"Bah!" Long Harry said. "And when we finally achieve such

understanding, the whole Universe will disappear in a puff of smoke."

"Could be," The Beak admitted. "Although, at our present rate, the Universe will have disappeared long before we begin to understand it."

"If there's anything more useless than philosophy, you tell me what it is," Long Harry said.

"Pointless action," The Beak told him.

"Nonsense. Taking direct action is always to be preferred to sitting around and speculating on the meaning of life. If you do something, even if it's the wrong thing, you'll have changed your situation. That makes it possible to do something else."

"That," The Beak said, "is a philosophy."

Long Harry grumbled.

The scroll keeper gathered us around him again after the last sack had been donned. "Let the record show," he announced, "that every person ('*pittel*,' a word meaning non-citizen, with an implied meaning of very dirty and not too bright) here is a direct slave, except only Roppa Pragrat sik Hummo Lik p'Froganno, the grotgraf. He is entered as a conditional slave, subject to his being ransomed within the assigned time. So it is written in the Lesser Scroll; so it shall be done." He rolled up the scroll and recapped it.

"Attention!" the other red-belt called. "I am the slavemaster. You will all receive your work orders from me, and if you have any questions or complaints you will address them to me. We will treat you fairly and without favoritism while you are here. Most of you will be sold at the next trading-time. I will demand discipline and conformity to our codes. I expect to be obeyed." He slapped his closed fist against his chest for emphasis while he spoke. "Oh yes, there is one thing. Will the one known as Tooka Fingal step forward?"

One of the cook boys took a few tentative steps, looking puzzled at being singled out.

"Tooka, our records show that it was in your personal chest that the six cuts of sheempja weed were found. In carrying and using this weed, you have violated the law and custom of the group you were traveling in. No violation of the law is permitted, and you must be punished. Have you anything to say?"

The kid looked around. "I...well, your honor, I...that is, I only...you see, I...."

"That is enough. Stammering is no defense. You are sentenced to ten lashes. Guards, strip him of his garment!"

Two guards came forward and pulled the sack over the confused boy's, head. He just stood there shivering and looking miserable.

"Administer the corrective punishment!"

One of the guards led the kid to a post and tied his arms around it. The other one uncurled a long whip from around his waist and measured off the appropriate distance. Then he turned and the whip hissed through the air. Ten lashes were counted off with an even stroke, leaving parallel welts across the kid's back. For the first few he didn't make a sound. At the fourth he screamed, and by the tenth he had sagged against his bonds and was crying uncontrollably. The guard wrapped himself back up in his whip and went back to his post without once changing the stern-but-fair expression his face had held all through this. The other guard cut the boy down, wrapped a clean cloth around his back, handed him his canvas sack, and then retreated in turn.

"That is all for now," the slavemaster said. "I will return with work assignments later." The trio turned and marched back over the drawbridge entrance, which was then raised.

"Well, well," Long Harry said. "I am surprised."

The Beak shook his head. "A psychological move to frighten us and keep us in line, that's all."

"I agree," Long Harry said. "And that's what I find surprising. Very neat, efficient, and effective these people are."

"How can you take it so calmly?" I demanded. "They seem to think that by keeping careful record they can excuse piracy, slavery and murder."

"It's an old syndrome," The Beak said. "People all through history have thought that 'I was only obeying orders' is sufficient excuse for whatever they do. I'd better go and see if I can do anything to help that lad."

CHAPTER TEN

The work we were put to was cutting a kind of hard peat from a bog right outside the settlement. The peat was then carted over to a pair of large kilns where it was turned into coke for use in the furnaces that supplied hot air to fill the balloons and in the braziers carried in the flying ships to keep the air in the balloons hot. The few women slaves were kept segregated at night, but ate the main meal with us, so it wasn't until noon the next day that we saw Thalla again.

"How are you all?" she asked, bringing her bowl of watery stew over to our bench. She was dressed in a plain, white cotton robe that hung down to the ankles and clung to her when she moved; a lot sexier and more comfortable than a canvas sack.

"We're fine," I told her. "What's been happening with you?"

"I'm fine too. When do we escape?"

"Have patience," Long Harry said.

"Are they treating you well?" The Beak asked.

"Very well. I'm under the protection of their Old Lady, since I'm a priestess. She's asking me a lot of questions about what I do, and all. She's very curious and she has a great talent."

"Old Lady?"

Long Harry wanted to know, "what sort of talent?"

"She's kind of the woman in charge of everything. The real boss is the Great Mother but she asks the Old Lady before she does anything. Then the Old Lady reads the portents in soup and entrails and things like that and tells her what to do."

"A matriarchy, I told you," The Beak said.

"Her talent is something else," Thalla continued. "She lifts things. Not real big things, but vases, dishes, things like that."

"Lifts things?" I asked.

"Yes. You know, without touching them. Just with her mind. She lifts things by thinking them up, and they go up."

"Telekinesis," Long Harry said in English.

"What's that?"

"That means lifting things by thinking about them," he explained.

"Yes. Well, that's what she does. She wanted to know if the Priestesses of Tor have any talents like that."

"Do they?" The Beak asked.

"Of course they do. That's how they get picked to be priestesses."

"You mean you can lift things?" I asked.

"Oh no. There are all sorts of talents. The only one I know I have is empathy. I know what people are feeling. Remember, I told you about it when I was teaching you Elsh. It's not very strong yet, but they're working on it. At least they will be if I ever get back."

"Don't worry," I told her. "We'll get you back."

"Look! Look up there!" Long Harry said, shielding his eyes against the sun and pointing up at the sky.

There, cutting a path neatly through the upper atmosphere of this backward planet was the contrail of a large jet transport.

"Wow!" I said. "How do you like that?"

"Oh, you see those all the time where I come from," Thalla said.

"Is that right?" The Beak asked. "Do you know what it is?"

"The common people say that it's a sign the gods are dividing the heavens among them but that's only superstition. It's some sort of natural happening, like lightning."

"Aha!" said Long Harry, shaking his finger at The Beak. "What do you say to that?"

"I say that if the gods had wanted us to know what it was, they would have labeled it."

Thalla went away confused.

That night we went about making friends with our fellow slaves and gaining their confidence, as Long Harry instructed. We each took a separate group. Mine were gathered under one umbrella, complaining.

"I hope they sell me fast. I don't fancy spending the rest of my life digging dirt."

"Don't worry, you won't live too long. That's hard work, and besides one of the plants or beasts'll get you 'fore too many weeks. Notice they's not many old-time slaves around this place."

"Gar! I'm sore all over. I think I'm sore in places I don't have."

"Yea. And, I'll tell you, if that guard comes over and tells me to dig faster one more time, I'll brain 'im with the friggin' shovel!"

"Sure, that'd be right smart. They'd whip you alive till you were dead."

"Well, anyway, it'd be a quick way to go."

"I don't think! They's damn good with those whips. They'd keep you alive as long as it suited them."

Then, while I was trying to figure out what to say to break into this cheerful conversation, one of them spotted me. "Say, what you lurking around here, fellow? Ain't you got your own blanket?"

"Har! Maybe as how he wants to crawl into yours. Maybe he's right soft; keep you both warm."

"Maybe so," the first allowed, eyeing me.

"Nothing like that, you guys," I whispered. "I just want to talk to you."

"Talk in the daylight; we need our sleep."

"I want to talk private."

"Right. Start talking. What you got to say?"

"Well, listen you guys; you want to stay here?"

"Nah!" one of them snorted. "I want to move into the palace at Grakel. I always been partial to palaces."

I was getting no place on a speeding pimpady. "That's not what I meant."

"Spit it out, what did you mean?"

"I mean escape. But maybe I'd better forget it, you guys sound like you're determined to stay here, why should I argue?"

"Escape? It's impossible to escape. There's no place to go."

"Right. Forget it. It takes guts and determination, and it might not work. It's dangerous and risky. Maybe you'd better stay slaves. They might sell you to someone who won't treat you too bad. Maybe make eunuchs out of you and stick you in some palace. Just forget it, I'll talk to someone else."

"Wait!"

"Yah, wait a minute. Tell us about this escape of yours."

"Are you interested?"

"Well, maybe so. Let's hear it."

"Not good enough," I told them. "It's my partner's scheme, and he says not to tell anyone unless they're in on it. The more people who know, the more chance for something to go wrong."

"How in the sacred name of the goddess of joy are we supposed to know if we're interested in it, if we don't know what it is?"

"That's a problem," I admitted. "It's like this: if you're interested enough in getting out of here to commit yourself to helping, then we want you and we'll explain your part; nobody but the boss will know the whole scheme, that way nobody can give it away. If you're only interested enough to talk about it, then we don't want you anyway."

"We're interested," one of them said. "What's the scheme?"

"You don't listen," I complained. "I'll tell you what; talk it over tonight and if you want to sign on, let me know tomorrow."

They agreed to that, and I crawled back to my blanket. Long Harry was waiting for me. "How'd it go?"

"I think they're hooked," I told him.

By three days later every *pittel* in the compound had agreed, and Long Harry was handing out work assignments. He still wouldn't tell us the details of his plan.

The next afternoon a shocking event occurred. I was stoking one of the furnaces and adjusting the long, leather tube that fed hot air into the gasbag of a patrol ship, when I heard a loud roaring sound. A few moments later a helicopter came into view and settled down in a clear space about a hundred yards from me. The other slaves around me were as shocked as I was, although their feeling was more one of supernatural dread. They hid behind any available structure or lay face down in the mud, and muttered a variety of incantations and prayers while making a variety of gestures to ward off the globular monster.

The pirates didn't seem at all alarmed. Our guard started kicking and prodding the prostrate forms around him, yelling "Come on, you superstitious bastards, get up and stoke the other furnaces before the fires go out. Haven't you ever seen a monster before?"

I decided to get a closer look at this one without seeming to want to, so I allowed myself to be prodded over to a cart and started pushing it toward a nearer furnace. When I got there, I checked to see that the guard was still busy with other recalcitrants, then darted behind a tent and snuck closer to the copter.

By this time it had shut its tip jets off, and the rotors were just whistling to a stop. Two men, dressed in black, very Earthy-type, one-piece jump suits, were sitting in the perviglass bubble.

Four of the pirates marched over to the ship, and one of the Earthmen got out. I found that I couldn't hear what they were saying from where I was, so clamping my teeth firmly down on my rapidly-beating heart, I wiggled around the tent flaps over to a closer tent and hid, prone, in its shadow.

"...more slaves?" one of the pirates was saying. "We don't have a very good selection right now. If you'd told us you were coming...."

"It isn't more slaves we're interested in," the Earthman said. "At least, not exactly. We're searching for three men that were probably on the last caravan you attacked. We didn't find out they were on that caravan until after it had left, and by the time we reached it all we found were a few burned wagons. That was your work, wasn't it?"

I was surprised they couldn't hear the pounding of my heart. I was sure I knew who the three men they wanted were.

"Us, indeed!" the pirate said proudly. "Which three men do you want?"

"We don't know what they look like. From the descriptions we got from the guards at the arena where they escaped, they're all twelve feet tall with great fangs, and lightning comes out of their fingertips."

The pirate laughed. "We don't have any slaves that would picture that way. They're all about three feet tall and they grovel a lot."

"These men will be easy to find," the Earthman said. "The one thing we're sure of is that none of them speak Elsh. Bring the men forward who don't know the language, and we'll sort them out."

"That should be easy," the pirate agreed. He sent one of his companions off for the slavemaster, who came strolling up a minute later. These pirates refused to be impressed.

"Ah, slavemaster. Our friends would like to buy three slaves."

"Very fine, very fine," the slavemaster said, rubbing his hands together. "Any special types, or just strong backs and weak minds as usual?"

"No, there are three special slaves that are wanted. From the crew we captured in that last pimpadigrot. Three particular slaves that don't speak Elsh."

"I'm sorry," the slavemaster said with a little bow, "but they can all speak. If you like, I can have their tongues ripped out. After about a week they should be recovered enough to work."

Cheerful mother.

"You misunderstand," the other told him. "They don't want slaves who can't speak, they want those who can't speak Elsh. Prisoners we captured on the last pimpadigrot who don't understand the language."

"But they all speak Elsh," the slavemaster said.

The Earthman glowered at him. "Are you sure?"

"Of course I'm sure. Both I and the scrollmaster spoke to them all when they were written into the Lesser Scroll."

"Did any of them speak very poorly, like with a bad accent?"

"A few of them had accents, but they all spoke the language well."

"They couldn't have learned the language so fast," the Earthman said.

"Perhaps someone taught them," the slavemaster offered.

"There was no one who spoke their language. Impossible!"

Bless Thalla and all her descendants.

"Then they just aren't here. Perhaps they were killed in the battle."

"You're not holding out?" the Earthman asked suspiciously.

"We're not what?"

"Keeping them back for some reason of your own."

"What reason would we have to keep men who couldn't speak the language? We'd have little use for them, and they'd be difficult to sell. Believe me, if there were such, we'd be pleased to pass them on to you—for the usual price."

The other Earthmen leaned out of the copter. "Maybe we're wrong," he said. "After all, if they can't speak Elsh, how could they sign up for the caravan?"

"But they couldn't be anywhere else after the way we searched. And that was the only caravan going out at the right time."

"Maybe they did something else. Or maybe, as our friend suggested, they were killed in the battle."

"We couldn't be that lucky," the first one said. He glowered around him and then climbed back into the copter. "If you run across anyone like that in, ah, your line of work, send word. We'll pay well, even for information."

"Agreed," the pirate said. "And when you need more plain ordinary slaves for your line of work, let us know." The Earthman growled something in reply, and closed the hatch. The tipjets roared to life, and the helicopter lifted and split.

* * * * * * *

That evening I reported the details of the exchange to my companions. It did not produce immediate joy. "They're closing in on us, and they seem very anxious to find us," Long Harry said. "I think we'd best get out of here as soon as possible."

"I don't plan to stay a day longer than necessary," The Beak assured him. "How do they know we're here?"

"I have no idea," Long Harry said. "I expect we'll find out eventually, only I hope it's on our terms and not theirs."

"We've got to fight them," The Beak agreed.

"How do we go about doing that?" I asked. "We're running from pillar to post. Every place we go we end up slaves."

"Our first job is to establish a secure base," Long Harry said. "Any tactician will tell you that."

"Sounds good," The Beak said. "How do we accomplish this weighty task, and what, exactly, does it mean?"

"In this case, we have to get to somewhere where we won't be persecuted for our race, religion, or previous condition of servitude. We need people who will listen to us."

"Where do we find all this?"

"Our young lady is the key to that, if we can get her back where she comes from. Her people may or may not listen to us, but they'll certainly accept us; and that's a first step."

"I think you have an interior motive," I said.

"Ulterior, and I don't. Our fellow Earthmen aren't up to any good on this planet, so it will help Thalla's people as well as us to do something about them."

* * * * * * *

The preparations for escape went ahead at what Long Harry assured us was a rapid rate. None of the men knew why they were doing any of the various things Long Harry set up, but they did them eagerly. The change in spirit was incredible. In fact, we had to give them morose lessons at night, or the pirates might have suspected something. As it was, the number of whippings went sharply up, and I learned the Elsh word for "recalcitrant."

The variety of different things going on was impressive. One crew was practicing the ancient and honorable art of sneaking up on guards and eliminating them every night. Another was assembling the largest logs they could find in one section of the bog while the guards' attention was drawn by another group that staged a variety of charades. We were all under instructions to swipe all the rope we could, and we spent long hours of the night tying and braiding the short pieces together.

One day, about two weeks later, Long Harry surveyed our work and found it good. He issued final instructions.

I spent the afternoon filling up the large barrel on stilts that served the pirates as a water tower. I contrived, as Long Harry said I should, to be just finishing when the whistle blew to order all slaves in for the night. I coiled the hose neatly and set it on a peg by the tower, instead of putting it away in the storage shed, and raced back to the compound like a good little slave.

We all sat around nervously, waiting for it to get dark. I stared at the sun, willing it to sink below the bog. "Say," I said, "I just realized something."

"What's that?" asked The Beak.

"I've been staring at the sun for the past five minutes."

Long Harry looked up from the diagrams he was drawing in the packed dirt. "Swell," he said.

"No, I mean, on Earth I couldn't do that. If you stare at the sun you'll go blind."

"So?" Long Harry encouraged.

"So shouldn't we be able to figure out what type star this is? I mean, like G1 or G3 or like that?"

"So?"

"So then we could tell where we are!"

"Nope," Long Harry said, and went back to his sketches.

"Why not?"

"In the first place," The Beak told me, "You could stare at

Sol if it was that low in the sky. In the second place, none of us know enough to determine what type star yon sinking sun is. In the third place, even if we could it wouldn't do us any good in the first place. There are many millions of stars of each type, and many thousands within the expanding sphere of our weave ship exploration. And in the third place—excuse me, the fourth place—even if we knew what star that was, how would it help us?"

"Well it works in all the books," I insisted.

One of the men came up and whispered, "Is it dark enough?"

"If I can see you," Long Harry told him, "It isn't dark enough. I see you."

"Why not call the meeting now," I asked. "They never check on us."

Long Harry lay back with his hands behind his head and his eyes closed. "Timing is important. I can't separate it out into sections in which timing is important and sections in which timing isn't so important; so timing is important for everything. Also, if I tell these men their jobs in advance they'll get nervous thinking about them."

"Everyone is nervous anyway," I told him.

"Hush," he said. I think he went to sleep for the next two hours, but I'm not sure. At any rate, he lay there without moving and The Beak went off in a corner and muttered to himself, leaving me to sit there and chew the stubs of my nails.

Someone was shaking me. I opened my eyes to the pitch dark of a night without a moon. If I looked up, there was a bright splatter of stars, but they did no good for looking straight ahead. "I'm not asleep," I said.

"Of course you're not," The Beak replied. "Wake up, the meeting's about to start."

Meeting is, perhaps, the wrong word. I think everyone had gathered around expecting a short, stirring speech or at least a few words of encouragement; you know: *In this dark hour...*, or, *When in the course of Human events...*or, *This is it, men; over the top at dawn!* or, *Grak expects every man to do his duty.*

What they got from Long Harry was, "Group leaders come here for your assignments; the rest of you shut up!"

When the group leaders had received their instructions, Long Harry stood up and surveyed the Slave Revolt. "If any of you get caught," he said, "pretend you're in it alone for as long as possible; that'll prevent the general alarm from being sounded. Don't do anything stupid."

That was Long Harry's final advice to the men, delivered in his usual flat, nasty tone. When I talk like that to someone, he hits me. I guess that's what leadership is. Some of the men attempted to cheer, but it was squelched by wiser heads. I could see it in the history books: "And then their great leader issued his immortal cry, which can be quoted by every schoolchild: 'Don't do anything stupid!'"

The men spread out into the general dark. Group one, our commando squad, prepared to go into action. They spread dirt and charcoal over their faces, arms and legs, then headed toward the far corner of the compound where they had hidden a two-log bridge and a stick and rope ladder in the dirty water of the moat. Their job was to eliminate the night guards in certain areas of the camp. Our job, again, was to wait. The Beak had made a crude timing device out of a pitcher with a small hole in the bottom, and we sat waiting while three pitchers of water dribbled out of the hole.

The suspense was very hard on the nerves. I sat waiting, occasionally sticking my hand under the pitcher to make sure water was still coming out, and listening for the first guard to scream or the general alarm gong to sound. The first year passed quickly, but the second took a while. Finally The Beak said, "Okay, it's time." Two runners went out to tell the other groups, and we headed toward our homemade exit.

As befitted the planners and leaders of this jailbreak, we were the last over the wall. We helped everyone else out first, making sure they understood what they were to do, and murmuring words of encouragement. The first group, all experienced swampmen, were taking coils of rope down to where they had been stashing all the logs they could find. They were to make a couple of rafts and pole their way to either oblivion or freedom. The second group was going to stoke up four of the hot air furnaces, which were always kept lit, and use two of them to fill the balloons on one of the skyships. The third group was going to raid the kitchens and bring supplies to the first two groups. The fourth group, us, had a more complicated task.

"We'll be the last to leave," Long Harry had explained, "and we'll need an edge."

"What sort of edge?"

"I think The Beak has given it to us. It's called water gas."

"Huh?"

"We'll use two of the furnaces to fill a balloon ship with water gas instead of hot air. It's lighter."

"Where do we get water gas?"

"We make it."

The Beak explained how, and after I had complained that it was too complicated, would take too long, and wouldn't work, I reluctantly agreed. That's what we were going to do.

After the last of the other groups had gone, I tiptoed across the rocking log bridge and clambered up the swaying rope ladder, with The Beak and Long Harry right behind me. The Beak and I then ran silently off to get water, while Long Harry strode purposefully to the furnaces to arrange the piping.

It was so dark that I had trouble keeping track of The Beak, who was only two steps in front of me. There was a small fire at the other end of the camp, with a few figures walking around by it; but all it served for was to illuminate itself and make some of the shadows seem even darker.

"Oof! What the...."

The Beak had bumped right into a guard that our commando squad has missed. "Oh, I'm sorry sir," The Beak said. "It was my fault, sir. I apologize, sir. I hope I didn't hurt you, sir." I knelt down and felt around for a rock.

"That's all right. Say, what are you doing...?" I clipped him on the back of the head with a small boulder I had found, and he dropped without further discussion.

"What'll we do with him?" I whispered.

"Leave him here, come on. And, thank you!" The Beak replied. We continued our tiptoe trot toward the water tower.

"Here it is," The Beak said, holding out his hand to stop me. "Where's the hose?"

"Around the side, on a peg. Here, I'll find it." With my left hand touching the framework, I stumbled around the water tower groping for the hose I had left there that evening. It didn't seem to be there, so I kept walking and feeling for it.

"What's the matter?" The Beak asked from right in front of me.

"What?" I stopped. "Oh, I must have walked all the way around. I guess I missed it; I'll try again." I groped around more slowly this time, keeping my hand high in the air to feel for the coils of hose. Maybe someone had removed them after I left? No—there they were, just higher up than I remembered. "Here!" I whispered.

"Wait a second," The Beak said, walking around the structure to where I was standing. "That's it? Good. Now, let's get busy. How do we get into this thing?"

"There's a ladder just a second—over here; here it is." I set the coils of hose on the ground, took one end and climbed the ladder. When I ran out of ladder, I straddled the top of the water tower and fed the hose down into the water until I was sure it had reached the bottom. Then I wedged it securely between the ladder and the tower and carefully climbed back down. "All secure," I announced.

"Fine. Now let's see if the scientific principle of the siphon works on this planet."

"Why shouldn't it?" I asked.

"Shut up," The Beak told me. He put the other end of the hose to his mouth and sucked at it until we heard a gurgling sound and little splatters of water came out, followed shortly by a steady flow. "Good!"

"There was always the chance," The Beak explained to me

in a gravelly whisper as we trotted the hose through the camp toward the first furnace, "that a leather hose wouldn't be air tight enough for the suction to work."

"What would we have done then?"

"You would have gone for a swim and filled the entire hose with water; it's very simple."

We reached the furnace and I watched the experts put theory to practice and assemble the water gas manufacturing plant. Long Harry was there waiting for us. The first furnace was going full blast, and he had fastened the hot air tube so that it went into the top chamber of the second furnace instead of into the balloon. We fastened the hose so that it would deliver a steady stream of water into the top chamber of the first furnace.

"You see," The Beak explained proudly, "this will boil the water. The steam will go down the tube to the second furnace. There it will pass over red-hot coke and pick up carbon atoms. The result, a mixture of molecular hydrogen and carbon monoxide, will fill the balloons. It'll give us a lot more lift than plain hot air."

"It sounds great," I said enthusiastically.

"Keep your voice down," Long Harry whispered.

"There's one thing," The Beak said. "We'll have to be careful."

"What of?" I asked him.

"Water gas is highly inflammable and poisonous." Long Harry looked up, his face glowing satanically with the reflection of the red-hot furnace. "Get the other tube in place," he instructed, "we're starting to get steam."

I climbed on board the ship we had picked. The Beak passed me the end of the tube, and I carefully placed it in the hot air orifice of the forward balloon, which was neatly furled for quick filling. As I came back to the rail, someone tapped me on the shoulder and I froze. My face broke out in an instant cold sweat and my hands felt clammy.

"Hello," Thalla said.

I straightened up. "You shouldn't sneak up like that," I told her. "If it had been anyone but me you would have really frightened him."

"Long Harry told me to sneak out and hide here until you came," she explained. "I must have been here for hours now. I was afraid you wouldn't come: that you'd been caught or that I was on the wrong ship or something. I'll try not to frighten you again. Are we going to escape? Now? I've brought all my things."

"We're getting ready now," I told her. "Just stay here."

"Hsst!"

I went over to the rail. "What is it?" I whispered into the darkness below.

"They've brought the food," Long Harry's voice floated up. "I'll hand it to you. You and Thalla stow it, then go around the ship and remove everything you can. We want this thing as light as possible."

"Right." We took the food on board, sticking the cloth-wrapped bundles in small bins under the seats. Then we went around collecting anything unnecessary and making a pile on the deck. There wasn't much. Various coils of rope and lengths of canvas I was afraid to remove, since I couldn't tell their function in the dark. There were several chests, a neat stack of shields, crossbows, grappling hooks and other, less identifiable, objects. When we had everything we could find in the pile, I climbed overboard and Thalla handed the stuff down to me. By this time the balloon was filling and the front end of the ship was starting to rock gently and show signs of wanting to lift off the ground.

Loud creaking noises and subdued murmuring sounded from behind the ship so, grabbing a spear, I went cautiously back to have a look. I could just make out the bulk of the ship behind ours lifting against its mooring lines. As I watched, the lines were cast free and the ship rose to be swallowed by the black sky.

Now I could hear noises from the camp. Not much louder than the regular night noises of the surrounding swamp, they were different enough to attract attention. To my oversensitive ears, they were as loud as cannon shots. I walked forward on the ship to find The Beak fastening the tube to the second balloon. "The other ship just left," I reported.

"Good, very good," he whispered back.

"What about us—how soon are we going to get out of here?"

The Beak finished fussing with the tube. "As soon as possible," he answered, rubbing his hands against his sides. "Within half an hour."

"Isn't it about time for a change of guard?" I asked. "We'll be spotted!"

"These people are Spartans," The Beak said. "One guard shift a night. With luck, they won't miss us until morning and by then we'll be long gone."

Long Harry climbed up the side. "The rafts have pulled out. We're the last ones left."

"Great," I said.

"Don't fret. Do the braziers on these craft have a grating above the fire?"

"I'll check," I said. I did. "Yes, they do."

"Excellent! There are sacks of coke and water bags by the side. Help me lift them on board." He leapt lightly over the rail and handed up this final cargo.

"The balloons are full," The Beak announced. We were now pulling steadily at our mooring lines, but still firmly anchored to the ground.

"Right. Pass down the tube and I'll go back and disarrange things so they won't figure out what we did. No use improving their technology." Long Harry took the end of the tube and disappeared.

* * * * * * *

"Rarg!"

A loud, angry yell came from across the camp. "Someone, ah, seems to have noted our absence," The Beak said. "Or, perhaps, he's stumbled over one of his colleagues."

"Let's get out of here!" I said, doing a good imitation of panic. *"Halloo! Halloo! Sound the alarm! Escape!"*

"Patience," The Beak said. "Plenty of time. Why don't you go around and locate all the mooring lines?" I stumbled around the deck, checking for lines and watching scattered lights spring up around the camp.

BONG BONG BONG TABONG

Long Harry returned and started climbing the side, then stopped. "Oh, hell!"

"What's the trouble? Come on up and let's get out of here!"

"I forgot something."

"What? Forget it, I'll buy you a new one."

"Fire. We can't leave without fire. Start casting off—I'll be right back." He dropped off the side.

We went around untying lines, leaving only four: two front and two back. The thing had been tied down better than Gulliver.

The gong had stopped now, but it wasn't needed any more. The whole camp was alert—or, at least, awake. People were rushing in all directions.

A glowing ember appeared waving in the air and heading toward us. It resolved into Long Harry, holding a coal in a pair of tongs and running all-out, closely pursued by a pair of half-dressed pirates waving swords. He reached the side off the ship and started climbing one-handed up to the rail. Both pirates grabbed for him. He kicked one aside, but the other got him around the knees.

Without conscious thought I launched myself over the rail and dropped feet first on the pirate's head. His neck snapped back and he fell to the ground like a sack of damp laundry. I landed on my knees on top of him and fell forward. Long Harry clambered over the rail, brandishing his precious lump of coal.

The second pirate, with the wind knocked out of him, gave up trying to find his sword in the dark and lurched at me. I kicked him in the face and rolled over, trying to get up. He fell on top of me and I struggled with him for a moment before I realized that he was unconscious.

Two more pirates were racing in, screaming, as I stood up. The last mooring line fell beside me and the ship lurched into the air. I stood, feet braced apart, to meet the pair as the ship rose over my head. There was a glint of light on the ground to my left that was probably a sword, and I tried to decide whether I could reach it before they reached me.

"Here!" Long Harry yelled from above me and a coil of rope fell by my feet, the other end fastened to the ship's rail.

I grabbed for the rope and was yanked into the air. It rose through my hands too quickly to hold, burning the skin off my palms. I fell about two feet and stumbled. Righting myself quickly, I reached for the coils of rope still on the ground and wound it twice around my chest under my arms.

I was heaved into the air just as one of the pirates reached me. He raised his sword to hack at either me or the rope, and I kicked him in the elbow. He screamed and dropped the sword. The other one arrived a second later. I was about fifteen feet off the ground and the end of the rope was just rising past him. He grabbed for it, just getting it by the tip, and was pulled into the air below me. He started climbing the rope hand over hand.

I was caught. Even if I was good at climbing ropes, which I'm not, I couldn't have gotten loose. The rope was wrapped twice around me and, with the pirate's weight pulling it tight below, I couldn't get it unwrapped. I was held as securely as if I'd been tied there, and the pirate was approaching.

"Help!" I yelled, jerking the rope back and forth to try and jar him loose. "Help!"

Long Harry's face appeared above me, peering over the rail. "Hang on a second!" he called.

"I have no choice," I yelled back. "Do something!" The pirate reached for my legs and I kicked at him. He retreated a few inches down, where I couldn't reach him, and worked at removing a long, triangular dagger from his belt.

"Here," Long Harry called. I risked looking up and saw a square, flat cleaver descending toward me at the end of a cord.

I grabbed for it and untied it. *Oh great,* I thought, *A fight to the death with knives on a rope suspended a couple of hundred meters above the ground.*

"Cut the rope!" Long Harry called.

The pirate was jabbing at my leg with his dagger. I swung the cleaver at him, causing him to back down, and then hacked savagely at the rope. It parted suddenly, and the pirate fell without a sound. I'm sure I would have screamed. The coil around my waist fell loose, and I almost followed the pirate but managed to grab hold just in time. Long Harry and The Beak pulled me up and I fell over the railing and collapsed in a happy heap on the deck.

CHAPTER ELEVEN

The next morning we had escaped the swamp and were flying over a broad, flat land planted in thin strips with something bearing bright blue flowers. I asked Thalla what it was, but she was a city girl. Far off in the distance, for the first hour or so after dawn, we could make out the small dot of another balloon ship, but it was too far away to tell whether it was fellow escapees or pursuers, and it soon disappeared.

"How far are we going to go?" I asked Long Harry.

"As far as possible," he said. "If we hit any large body of water we'll have to come down instead of trying to cross it, but if not we'll just keep going until we run out of gas."

The live coal that Long Harry had brought aboard with such trouble last night had been used to light the braziers. The grates on top of them were filled with coke, which we kept damp, and the whole contraptions were placed below the bottom holes of the balloons. The idea was, The Beak explained, that the damp coke would keep the balloons filled with a combination of steam, water gas, and hot air, and prevent the inflammable mixture in the balloons from going up. I hoped he was right but the fire looked all too close to the holes to suit me.

For a while we tried fooling with the sails but we couldn't get any noticeable results from them so we soon gave up. By early afternoon, with no sign of pursuit behind us and nothing to do but drift along, we had turned into a sightseeing party. There was nothing much to see but we worked at it. It was better than the swamp.

"Look at that rock," I said.

"Where?" Thalla demanded. "Show me!"

The Beak came over "You see a rock?"

"There, over there," I pointed.

"Yes, I see it. You're right, it is a rock," Thalla said. We all stared at the rock as if it were the Taj Mahal or the ruins of Los Angeles. Long Harry was too good for such sport. He kept himself busy estimating our ground speed and computing our height and keeping records with a piece of charcoal on a flat board. Occasionally he would make an Announcement, like: "I estimate our present ground speed to be about thirty-five knots," or "I compute our present altitude to be about four hundred meters." We were all properly impressed, although I didn't really think it mattered much.

Later that afternoon we were treated to some scenery worth looking at, if you like that sort of thing. We flew over an Army in full costume and complete with all equipment. Their technology was about on a par with the Romans', and we got a good view of such things as siege machines, battering rams, onagers, arquebuses, war towers and the like. They had one tremendous long tube that might have been a cannon but I couldn't be sure.

We caused a lot of excitement among the soldiers below, but they didn't seem particularly frightened by the ship. Some of them waved at us and some fired an arrow or two, each according to his temperament, I suppose. The arrows fell far short. One commander, on spotting us, had his entire company hide under their shields. The Beak thought he must be superstitious, but Long Harry insisted that he was just taking the opportunity to give his men training in an unusual tactic.

When dusk fell, we were noticeably lower and running out of fuel for the braziers. "Perhaps we should land this craft before it gets too dark," The Beak suggested.

Long Harry surveyed the situation. "You're right," He agreed. "Put out the fires, and we'll look for a suitable place to put down."

One place looked as good as another to me, since the entire

country below was perfectly. flat, but I didn't say anything. Long Harry had done a creditable job of commanding this expedition up to now and I was perfectly happy to let him continue. I unstowed a couple of canvas buckets and Thalla and I held them while the Beak filled them from the water bags. There was no way to put them down, as they would have collapsed.

We each tossed our bucket of water over one of the braziers, producing great clouds of steam,. and went back for refills. The second buckets produced even more steam, but by the third the coals just sat there and sizzled.

"We're going up again," Long Harry called from the prow. "Are the fires out?"

"Just about," I told him. We tossed another bucket on them, using up the last of our water, and I went to the rail to look over the edge. We were indeed going up. I could see the ground noticeably shrinking below.

"What's happening?" I asked. "Shouldn't we be going down?"

Long Harry clumped aft. "That steam must have lightened the balloons," he said. "But the effect should wear off in a minute."

"It's worse than that," The Beak volunteered. "I think we've hit a temperature inversion layer. The air here is quite a bit colder. We'll have to let some of the gas out of the balloons."

"How do you do that?" I asked.

"There should be a valve. See if you can find it."

We walked all around the two balloons, looking for some way to let the gas out, but we couldn't find it. "We could cut holes in the fabric," I suggested.

"If we tear the fabric, the rent will probably continue up the side, letting all the gas out at once and causing us to fall with some velocity to the ground," The Beak informed me. "I don't suggest it."

By this time it was starting to get dark. "What do you suggest?" I asked.

The Beak shrugged. "Trust to luck," he said. "I don't see that we have much choice. We'll land sometime during the night. If we're over water, the boat will float. We'll cut the balloons free and drift till morning."

Long Harry looked disconsolate. One of his plans wasn't working out perfectly. "Cheer up," I told him. "Freedom, even on a drifting boat, is better than slavery. We've done better than any of us had any right to hope for."

Long Harry glared at me, growled something, and stalked off.

We salvaged enough hot coals from one brazier to heat up some of the cured meat and ate it between slabs of hard cheese, washing it down with the remains of the water. It grew pitch-dark.

In about an hour we passed over a curved line of campfires, going from left to right like pearls on a great necklace. We seemed to be getting lower again.

Fifteen minutes later, we struck something, scraped along it for a minute and then bobbed free.

"Quick," Long Harry called. "Get knives. The next time we hit, cut the balloons loose. Otherwise, we'll be pulled along the ground for miles."

I picked up the meat knife. "Suppose it's the side of a mountain?" I asked.

"Take a chance," Long Harry said. "Life is a series of small risks."

We touched down again, and the ship started dragging along sideways. Holding onto the rail for support, I hacked away at the balloon lines on my side. With a final lurch the ship lay gently over on its side as the balloons, ropes dangling, lofted away.

"Well," I said. "We're down, we're safe and we're free. That's something."

"All right in there," a voice called out, sternly in Elsh. "You're surrounded. Come out peacefully."

"Shit!" Long Harry said.

We helped each other over the side of the ship and climbed down.

"Where are we?" Thalla called.

"You're in the city of Beloparsus. I'm the Commander of the Guard on the East Wall. Is that a girl?" Footsteps crunched across the gravel, and a shaft of light sprang up and focused on us. "Are there only four of you?"

"Yes," Long Harry assured him. "And we come in peace."

"As to that, you have little choice. You are my prisoners."

Thalla clapped her hands. "The Moving City! What luck! I had no idea we were anywhere near the River Belo. Captain, I am a Priestess of Tor and these are my friends."

The footsteps and the light came closer. "Can you prove that, young lady?"

"I have been a prisoner in Grak and a captive of the marsh pirates, whose vessel we stole to make our escape. My Amulet of Rank and Authority was taken from me in Grak, but if you will notify the local temple they can send for someone to vouch for me."

"It is a strange tale you tell," the captain said. "Escape from Grak and then from the marsh pirates by stealing a balloon ship." He crunched up to us and shone a lantern in each of our faces in turn. "Aren't you a little young to be a priestess?" he asked Thalla.

"I found my vocation early," Thalla said. "If you send for one of the Sisters, I'm sure she can identify me."

"The hour is too late to disturb the temple," the captain said. He put his hand to his chin and thought deeply for a minute, then came to a decision. "Come with me. I won't put you in prison but I'll give you quarters to sleep in this night. Under guard, of course. We'll straighten this out in the morning."

"Fair enough, Captain," Long Harry said.

We had landed on the roof of a large, low building, some sort of storehouse. The guards, alerted by our scraping across the wall, had been waiting for us. The ship was placed under guard and the captain escorted us across to another building where we were each given a separate small room, with a guard posted at each door.

It was the nicest confinement I had been in for a long time. The bed was soft, the blankets thick and warm, and I was asleep within five minutes after my head hit the feathered pillow.

The next morning new wonders awaited us. Baths! I soaked in the hot water for an hour and scrubbed myself all over several times before I started to feel clean again. I was ready to drain the water out and start over when, with a polite knock at the door of the bathing chamber, someone informed me that my new clothes were laid out and I should dress for breakfast.

Beloparsus treated its guests very well. The clothes were a sort of undress guard's uniform: black tights, black boots, a kind of baggy shorts and loose-fitting cotton shirt in light grey. Over this was a belted grey tunic with silver edging and a row of large, silver buttons up the side. The belt was designed to support a sword, but none was provided, which was reasonable since we were still, technically, prisoners.

My two companions were similarly garbed when I met them at breakfast although Long Harry's clothes were at least one size too small for his long frame. Thalla was in a knee-length, pleated red dress with a high collar and long sleeves trimmed in some sort of fur. She had on very pretty black shoes with pointy toes and block heels. Where the guards had procured clothes for her I didn't know and decided not to ask. She had very well-shaped legs.

Breakfast was in the officer's mess on a long table with a tablecloth and real ceramic plates. The officer who discovered us ate with us and was very friendly but I noticed that there were guards standing casually by all the exits.

After breakfast (cereal, meat, eggs, a sweet-tasting milk and bitter tea), Captain Lebipro escorted us to the Temple of the Sisters of Tor the Mighty. The city of Beloparsus had narrow, dusty streets with wooden sidewalks crammed full of small shops and stalls. Although it was still early, the streets were crowded with merchants and customers. About every fourth person I saw was in some sort of uniform.

The temple was a three-story, square building without

windows. Inside it was divided into a maze of small rooms and twisting corridors. Lighting came from frosted glass panels set into the ceiling. The sisters greeted us politely, obviously expecting us, and led us into a small waiting room. Thalla went off with them.

"Priestesses," I commented, watching their miniskirted posteriors oscillate down the corridor as they walked Thalla to her meeting with the Resident Mother, "shouldn't dress like that."

"That's not, ah, a very religious perfume they're wearing either," Long Harry said, sitting far down and trying to pull his shirt sleeves down far enough to button the cuffs.

"Delightful girls, the Sisters," the Captain said, stroking his pointed beard, "excellent company anywhere." He looked at us. "They all have the Talent, you know, in one form or another. Why do you think it is that people with the Talent all seem to combine it with a sort of refreshing innocence?"

"I don't know," I said.

"Fascinating city you've got here," Long Harry said.

"Yes. We don't get many tourists in the moving city but those who come find it so."

"The moving city? That's what Thalla called it last night," The Beak said. "How did it get that name?"

"You don't know the story of Beloparsus?" the Captain asked, sounding surprised. "Its fame must not be as widespread as I had thought. Beloparsus, furthest outpost of the Parsintan Empire—surely you've heard of the Parsintan Empire—established on the Belo River across the Eastern Sea from Parsint some two-hundred years ago. Under siege by the Urgazteth Confederation for the last sixty years, Beloparsus has never surrendered, but has been fighting its way down the river to the sea. An example of courage and determination for freemen everywhere."

"Why?" Long Harry asked.

"What?"

"Why have you been fighting your way down to the sea?"

"Because the river has been silting up and we can't get dredges out. We depend on the supplies brought up river by the merchant service and on the Parsintan Navy to keep the sea and river open."

"Yes, but why haven't you just pulled out?"

"Retreat?"

"Call it a strategic withdrawal."

"Desert?"

"Fight your way out against impossible odds, in what would surely be one of the great feats of the Parsintan Navy. Ballads would be written, statues would be erected...."

"We can't do that."

"Why not?"

"Because of our bases to the south. Beloparsus is needed as a way station."

"Ah!" Long Harry said. "Now we understand. Such industry is indeed noble when in a practical cause."

"Sixty years!" The Beak said. "You've really been under siege all that time?"

"The whole time. Of course the amount of strength the Urgaztethians can bring against us varies from time to time. There was the False Siege of the Pekkadomites, where for two years we could almost come and go as we pleased, then there were the time of the Battle of the Tunga Crop and the attacks of the Filbians and the Tenth Legion of Urgazteth. Those were all before my time. A mere two years ago, right before I made Captain, there was a storming of the North Gate, when the Logoth Cavalry actually made it past the first defense and up to the main gate. That was a bad week. We were in the midst of a major creep, and I guess we'd gotten sloppy, it had been so long since we were seriously threatened. They caught us just at the wrong time. Heads rolled, I can tell you. Several section commanders were relieved and sent back to Parsint before their tours were up, and the courts-martial went on for four months."

The Beak looked interested and rubbed the tip of his nose. "Tell me, if it doesn't violate military security, exactly how does

Beloparsus move?"

"Well...." Captain Lebipro stood up and started pacing back and forth, his hand stroking his beard. "It's a complex process, you realize, very much like a ritual dance. You know: stug, bela, once around, Parsek, and decompose.

"The first stage is the clearing of the area. This is done with cannonade and cavalry, used alternately. Second is taking the ground: infantry, along with sappers, engineers and auxiliaries are used here. Then filling the land and moving the outer or movable walls into place. The inner, or first fixed wall, can be moved any time after that, although it is usually done within the next two weeks. Sometimes the final, or small, wall is moved, sometimes it is left as a city defense and a new one built.

"After a certain amount of Westland is taken, a similar section of Eastland is relinquished. Thus the city of Beloparsus moves toward the sea."

"I see," The Beak said. "It sounds fascinating."

"Would you like to observe the process in operation? I think that could be arranged if, ah, ahem...." He left the rest unsaid. What he meant was, if we got a clear bill from the Sisters of Tor.

"Thank you," The Beak replied. "We would like that very much. When would be convenient—that is, if we don't end up visiting the inside of one of your jails?"

The Captain looked embarrassed. "Well...any time after tomorrow. I'm being officially relieved of duty tomorrow and it'll be about a week before my ship sails, so I'll have a good amount of free time."

"Your ship? Then you're not from Beloparsus?" I asked.

"I am an officer in the Second Regiment of the Imperial Parsint Guard. We all serve rotating tours of duty at Imperial outposts. I've been here six years and now I go home for at least four years. After that, back to some other far-flung outpost station. Part of the Thin Grey Line, you know."

One of the Sisters came for us then, and we clenched wrists with Captain Lebipro and departed.

The Resident Mother, a short, fat woman with lively eyes,

was sitting balanced in the center of a gigantic, circular red cushion in her reception room. Thalla sat on a small, square cushion by her side. The room was thickly carpeted and hung with yard after yard of varicolored drapes. Mother was wearing a loose-fitting tent of bright red that made her, at first glance, look like an outgrowth of the cushion.

"Welcome," she said, waving us forward. "Thalla has told me of your many adventures and of how you rescued her. On behalf of the Sisterhood, I thank you. You are brave and valiant men."

"It was nothing," Long Harry said, with an "any heroes would have done the same" shrug.

The Beak nodded. "She was at least as much aid to us as we were to her. Probably more."

The Resident Mother looked around her, puzzled, and then lifted a stray fold of her dress aside, revealing a gold platter resting on the cushion. "Ah, there it is!" She helped herself to a couple of dark brown, candy balls from the tray and then offered some to us. They were very light and seemed to be made principally from sugar and alcohol. I had two.

"Well, little Sister," Momma said, "these gentlemen think well of you."

"I didn't do much," Thalla insisted. "I think the one useful thing I was able to do was teach them Elsh."

"They didn't speak Elsh?" Mother asked. "You must be a good teacher. They speak it quite well now."

"That's part of the story I wanted to tell you after you called them in," Thalla said. "It's very curious. They have a strange history and come from a faraway place. Very far away."

"The Southern Islands?" the Resident Mother asked, looking us over. "Freeman Beak is dark and short, like a Southern Islander, but these other two don't fit in there. The tall one, Freeman Longharry, doesn't look like he comes from anywhere on this world."

"How did you know?" Thalla asked.

"What's that, dear?"

"I first found out when I heard them speaking the sacred language in the cells."

Now she had the Resident Mother's complete attention. "They speak the sacred language?"

"We do," Long Harry told her. "We call it English."

"That's very interesting," Mother said, reaching behind her to pull on a hanging cord. "You'll have to tell me all about that."

"Well," Long Harry said, "The way we see it...." Four large guards, swords drawn, raced into the room. I froze, awaiting developments.

"Surround them!" the Resident Mother rapped, pointing a plump, accusing finger at us. The guardsmen arranged themselves around us, swords pointing inward.

The Beak groaned and sat cross-legged on the floor. "I should have expected it!"

"Now look—" Long Harry said, taking a step forward and being stopped by the point of a sword.

"You don't have to jab that thing at me," I told a guard facing me. "I'm not going anywhere."

Thalla gasped. "What does this mean?" she asked the Resident Mother. "Why are you doing this?"

"You aren't supposed to know," Mother told her kindly, "and it must be a shock, but anyone outside the order who speaks the sacred language must be regarded as an enemy." She turned to us. "Why did you mislead the girl? Your surely didn't think you'd be able to fool me after I'd heard, did you?"

"I don't know what you're talking about," Long Harry stated firmly.

"Right," I agreed. "Me either. What are you talking about?"

"Surely there's no need to maintain the pretense any longer," Mother said. "I know that you must be Priests of Kallo." She smiled sweetly. "Of course you will not be allowed to leave this building, considering what you know. We will treat you as humanely as possible—considering."

"Considering what?" The Beak asked quietly from his seat on the floor.

"Considering the fact that you possess information that we surely must get out of you and considering the way you treat our people."

"I still don't know what you're talking about," Long Harry reiterated. "You're making some sort of mistake."

"With the greatest respect, I would like to agree," Thalla said. "These men are not our enemy."

The Resident Mother started speaking. For a second I didn't understand her, then I realized she was speaking English. "It must have been quite a shock to you when this innocent child spoke in your language," she said. "You didn't know that anyone not of your murderous group knew it. You must not be allowed to leave with that secret."

The Beak held up a forefinger mildly. "Am I to understand," he asked, switching back to Elsh, "that only these, ah, murderous Priests of Kallo speak this language we call English?"

"Of course," Mother insisted. "Do you deny it?"

The Beak shrugged. "It follows, then, that you and Thalla are also Priests of Kallo."

"Don't be foolish," Mother yapped. "We learned it separately."

"So did we," The Beak said.

"Hmm? Can you prove that? I'm willing to listen before I lock you up."

"Thalla knows our story," The Beak said. "I'll let her tell it, then if you have any questions I'll try to answer them."

The Resident Mother looked down at Thalla. "Go ahead, girl, tell me what these men told you. Don't be nervous."

After what Thalla had been through in the past week, it would have taken more than a short, plump Resident Mother to make her nervous. She rested her hand against one exposed knee, tapping her fingers in time to an inner rhythm. "The stars," she began, "are not really stars. They are really suns, like our own, with little planets going around them."

"That's been accepted theory for the past hundred years, girl. No lectures on elementary astrology, please."

"This one begins the same," Thalla told her, "but it ends different." She went on to tell the Resident Mother what The Beak had told her back in the cell: about our being from another planet where English is a common language, and about the transmatter, and how we'd ended up in the arena through some mistake that we didn't understand. The Beak didn't seem to have mentioned why we were being transported. Thalla had the impression we were some sort of tourists.

Somewhere around the middle of the narrative the Resident Mother got interested. She leaned forward and listened intently, absentmindedly nibbling candies from the tray.

"Fascinating!" she said when Thalla's narrative dribbled to a close. "That would explain a lot too. It surely would. But, there's one point: everything they told you could be true with the simple change that it was a receiving device in the Temple of Kallo in Parsint they were originally, ah, aimed for."

"But then—" Thalla began.

"I know. But then they surely wouldn't have had any reason to tell you the truth and they would have been much more upset at your speaking the sacred language."

"That's not what I was going to say," Thalla told her. "What I was going to say was: but then they wouldn't have had any reason to hide when those other Earthmen showed up."

"Other Earthmen? When was this?"

"At the pirate's camp," Thalla told her. "They came down in a big, mechanical flying thing and asked for prisoners who didn't speak Elsh. My friends hid from them until they left."

The Resident Mother thought deeply about this, her hand moving absently in a cycle from the golden tray to her mouth. When her groping hand found that she had run out of bonbons, she folded it in her lap and leaned forward. "Have any of you three anything to say?"

"If there are renegade Earthmen in this Temple of Kallo," Long Harry said, "we might be able to help you."

"You have already helped," Mother said. "I believe your stories. There are several facts that haven't been mentioned that tip the weighing pans strongly in your favor. For one thing: all the priests of Kallo speak perfect Elsh. I have Thalla's word that she had to teach you the language and I don't think she could be fooled about a thing like that. Our girls are well trained in the language arts." She raised her hand and eyes to the guards. "You may go—you won't be needed."

The guards each took a step backward, sheathed their swords, and trotted briskly out of the room.

"Thank you, Mother," The Beak said. "There are some questions...."

"Yes, and I have some for you. But surely they can wait until tomorrow. I need time to think this out. The implications of what you have already told me need sorting out. The rooms you used last night will be held for you. I shall so direct. You are now, with your permission, agents of the Temple of Tor. I shall give instructions that you are to be paid an advance so that you can purchase needed items."

"That's very good of you," The Beak said.

"Not at all," The Resident Mother said, smiling. "I think you'll earn the silver. You may go now. Please return tomorrow at the time of the triple horn. Thalla will, of course, stay."

CHAPTER TWELVE

Captain Lebipro grinned at us over his breakfast eggs the next morning. "I'm glad to see everything worked out well," he said

"So are we," I told him. I was feeling particularly contented, having gotten a haircut and shave the afternoon before and soaking for an hour in an oil-scented bath in the evening. The barber had left me with a close-cropped beard and the start of a fine moustache, so I was feeling particularly dashing. He had also sold me a wicked looking straight razor and a stropping leather, complete with brush, soap and wooden traveling case. I was all set to slit my throat in style. Long Harry had insisted that we spend part of our advance on three plain but serviceable swords, but even with that I still had a few coppers in my purse.

"We've been examining that flying ship of yours," Lebipro said. "It's fascinating. We'd heard reports of them but this is the first one any of us has actually seen. Our balloon expert was practically crying as he took this one apart. We use tethered balloons for observation quite a bit, but nothing like that."

"It is quite impressive," The Beak agreed. "It's surprising that a bunch of pirates, whose civilization is so low in other respects, would be able to maintain the technology."

This was obviously a new thought for the Captain. He pondered it for a moment, and then dismissed it. "The balloon-master would like very much to speak with you," he said. "The concept of controlling the flight of balloons interests him very much; he'd like to hear from you how the various sails and ropes are used to vary speed and direction."

"There's very little we could tell him," Long Harry said, putting down his tea and wiping his moustache carefully with the napkin. "We didn't get much chance to watch the ships in use, and when we did, I'm afraid we were preoccupied. We didn't steer the thing at all."

"We did use a superior lifting gas," The Beak added. "If your balloonmaster is interested, I'd be glad to explain that to him."

"I'm sure he'll be fascinated," the Captain said. "I'll tell you what—I have to get the Sergeant-Major to sign my equipment release form, then I'm officially off duty until my ship sails. I could give you that tour we spoke of and find the balloonmaster for you. We're scheduled to start a creep today. You might find it interesting."

"Sounds like fun," Long Harry said.

"Remember," The Beak said, "we have an appointment with Mother at the time of the triple horn."

"No problem," Captain Lebipro insisted. "I'll see you make it on time."

We left the breakfast table and trooped down the hall. At the first turn I got tangled in my sword and almost tripped.

"You, ah, don't wear swords where you come from?" Captain Lebipro asked, trying not to laugh.

"Not very often," I admitted. "What am I doing wrong?"

"You'll find that the sword will be much easier to handle if it hangs straight up and down from the belt," he told me.

"But I'm sure I've seen them like this," I said, adjusting the scabbard to the fore and aft position I was using.

"Perhaps," he said, "but not with that rigging. This chain is meant to fasten to the belt here, and this one over here, and the sword will hang straight. Look around."

I did, and sure enough, all the other swords were hung as he suggested. I don't know why I hadn't noticed it. I immediately undid the belt and refastened the sword scabbard. It hung quietly in place after that, and didn't get in the way.

Our first stop was the Guard Commander's office, where the

Captain got his release papers signed so he was officially off duty. Then we headed over to a tower that abutted the inner wall, a part of that collection of walls, battlements, ditches and towers that made up the East Wall Defense Group.

The second floor of the tower was one large room, over which the bits and pieces of our pirate ship had been disassembled and spread out. In one corner, muttering over a gas flame and a bit of fabric, was a tall, extremely thin man, wearing the first pair of spectacles I had seen on this planet—two thick, completely round lenses in a complicated wire frame that fit over his head and was fastened at the back of his neck.

"Good Morning, Master Grubb," Captain Lebipro called. "Allow me to present to you the gentlemen who arrived in this contraption you're so busy examining."

"Aha!" Master Grubb said, putting down the cloth and striding across the room. "Good of you, very good...." He grabbed each of us by the hand and pumped it up and down. "There are a few things...," he mumbled, pulling Long Harry back across the room with him. "Here, for example, this knot...." He picked up a hunk of rope and waved it in Long Harry's face. "Why do you use this instead of a running toe-bite or a double cleat? Or the fabric of the balloon envelope, here. Ouch! I forgot, it's hot. What is the composition of the coating?"

"Long Harry smiled and shook his head. "I'm sorry, I can't tell you."

"Come now," Master Grubb said. "Just a hint? Is it vegetable or mineral?"

"He didn't mean he won't tell you," The Beak said. "He meant what he said. He can't tell you. He doesn't know."

"Can't? Doesn't?"

"We stole the ship," I explained. "We don't know anything about the way it was made or used. I'm sorry."

Grubb's face sagged. "Ah well. It's a shame. Back to the burner and the crucible."

"I might be able to help you in one way," The Beak suggested.

"Yes? What's that?"

"What sort of gas do you use now to lift your balloons?"

"Muffleflem."

"I don't know the word."

"Here, I'll show you." Master Grubb took a handful of metal filings from a can and put them into a tall, thin glass beaker. Then he carefully poured a colorless fluid from a glass-stoppered bottle over the filings. The mixture immediately started bubbling. Taking a slender wax taper from a holder on the table, he lit one end in the gas flame and held it over the bubbling beaker.

PHEEEP!

A light blue flame filled the beaker momentarily, blowing the taper out as it escaped into the room. "Muffleflem," Master Grubb said. "The lightest gas we know."

"Hydrogen," The Beak said. "I don't think we can help you after all. Sorry about that."

Master Grubb shrugged. "Rediscovery is, after all, easier than discovery. At least you're sure that there is an answer."

We left him holding the square of cloth back over the gas flame and muttering softly to himself.

A soft, booming sound reached us as we left the tower, like the beating of a distant bass drum. "What is that?" I asked. "Some sort of signal?"

"It's the start of the cannonade at the other end of the East Wall. The creep is about to begin. Come along and we'll take a look."

I felt like telling the Captain that going to take a close look at the start of a battle wasn't exactly my idea of a morning's fun, but The Beak looked interested, and Long Harry looked positively eager, so I kept my mouth shut.

"How far away is it?" Long Harry asked.

"About thirty blocks South, near the river."

"It's quite a walk, let's get started."

"We don't walk," Captain Lebipro told us. "As guests of the Guard, we get to use the rope carriage."

"The who?" I asked.

"Come along."

We passed through a gate in the Great Wall, and walked up to the second outer wall. Climbing up a flight of stairs in its side, we entered a door about two-thirds of the way up its fifty-foot height. Inside the door was a long platform fronting what looked like a horizontal ski lift. The platform was about ten feet wide, and ended with a sheer drop to the floor below. In front of the platform was a continuously moving line of wooden benches hooked by metal poles to a thick cable about ten feet above. Across the way was another platform with its endless line of benches moving the other way. The. place was filled with a continuous clattering noise.

"The rope carriage," the captain said. "Our way of getting troops where we need them fast. Hop aboard." There were, I noticed, occasional men riding the benches as they pulled out of the station,

"How?" I asked.

"It's simple." The captain swung himself aboard one of the benches, rode about ten feet with it and swung off. "Nothing to it."

"Let's go!" Long Harry said. He and The Beak hopped aboard a passing bench. The Captain grabbed the next.

Trying hard not to look down, I stepped off the platform onto the next bench and sat down. It swayed alarmingly to the side, and I grabbed for a pole. After a second it stopped swaying, and I felt better, although it remained about fifteen degrees off center.

"What powers this thing?" The Beak called.

"The river," the Captain answered.

"How?"

"How should I know? I'm a soldier, not an engineer."

My bench gave a lurch, a bump and a thump. I looked up. The rope had just passed over a connector. They hung down from the roof every twenty feet or so, and thumped when the bench poles went through them. That explained the clattering noise.

As we rode the booming noise crept under the clattering and gradually got louder until at last the clattering was merely background noise for the roar of the cannon.

"We get off here," Captain Lebipro yelled as another station came into sight. We all leaped for the platform, and I managed to make it without falling.

As we approached the forward wall, the booming of the cannon got so loud that it was hard to think, then, all of a sudden, it stopped.

"What was that?" I said.

"The cannonade has ended," the Captain said. "It's either a cavalry sweep or an infantry advance, depending on how strongly these siege trenches were held. Let's get up to the top of the wall where we can see."

The forward wall was twenty feet high, and of rough stonework. As we got near I could see that it was hollow and resting on a stone-slab platform. The top was made up of thick, wood-beam platforms for the guns, set about twenty feet apart, with wooden walkways between them.

We climbed up a ladder to one of the gun positions, where a lieutenant gave a casual open-hand salute to Captain Lebipro and welcomed us aboard.

The thick gunpowder smoke which covered the forward area was just starting to. clear, and I could make out figures running back and forth somewhere in front.

"Infantry attack?" the Captain asked.

The lieutenant snorted. "Just cleaning out the area," he said. "Hardly any opposition at all. These new cannon must have scared them away."

The gun platform held two cannon, each of which was a great iron tube resting on a massive, wheeled wooden carriage. The wheels were iron shod and set in tracks, which were in turn mounted on a platform. that could be turned from side to side to aim the gun. Elevation was achieved by a row of holes up the side of the carriage. The gun would be wedged up to the required height and then secured by iron pegs run through the holes.

"The latest thing," the lieutenant told us. "The muzzle-loader is obsolete."

"These aren't muzzle-loaders?" The Beak asked as we stepped forward to examine the near cannon.

The gun was open-breach, with a wide chamber which narrowed down to a bore about twice the size of a man's fist. The lieutenant patted the side proudly, while he explained how the thing worked. First either a ball or a canister of shot was loaded into the chamber and rammed up the bore. Then a machined-metal jug holding the powder was set into the opening and pushed forward so that its neck fitted tightly in the chamber. A large screw-plate was tightened to hold the jug in place and a curved metal bar was locked on top. The gun was fired through a touch-hole in the jug. The gun could be fired as rapidly as new shot and powder jugs could be set in place.

"The technology is impressive," Long Harry said, inspecting the screw mechanism.

"It's more than impressive, it's impossible," The Beak replied.

"What do you mean?"

"These powder jugs aren't cast iron, they're machined steel."

"Of course," Long Harry said. "Cast iron that thin couldn't contain even a black powder explosion. The thing would explode like a grenade."

"Does it occur to you that this is the only example of high-grade alloy work we've seen on this planet?"

I picked up one of the jugs and examined it. It had a shiny finish and seemed to have been made all in one piece, but I didn't know enough about metals to tell more than that. Then I turned it over. It had printing engraved on the bottom. I read it and thought about it for a minute. I was not fond of my conclusions. "Harry! Beak! Come here and look at this!"

"What is it, Daniel?" The Beak asked, as they came over to examine my find. I pointed to the letters:

Dortmund & Essex
Geheime Spezial 13496
Neues Reich ° ° ° pruf

"Aha!" The Beak said. Long Harry was silent.

"These guns are very impressive," I told the captain. "Where do they come from?"

"They've been shipped over direct from Parsint for about the last six months," he told me. "I believe they're made in the armory of the Priests of Kallo, but I'm not sure. The Temple of Kallo has been coming out with a lot of new things in the past two years."

"I'll just bet," The Beak said.

[I'd like to point out here that our command of Elsh wasn't nearly as good as I've made it seem. I've left out a lot of pointing at things and grunting, waiting for the word to be supplied.]

When we left the front the area had just been declared secure, and the first wall. was being jacked up and rollers slid under. Teams of pimpadies were waiting behind the wall to be put in harness and drag the wall to its new location.

Captain Lebipro accompanied us to the temple, leaving us there with a promise to keep in touch.

We were taken into a different room this time. A massive rectangular table, surrounded by straightback chairs with ornately carved arms and legs, took up most of the space. The only hanging was a great tapestry depicting a variety of mythological beasts without the slightest attempt at perspective, which covered one wall. I realized, after staring at the tapestry for some time and admiring the lush colors, that on this world the beasts might not be mythological.

The Resident Mother was joined at her place at the head of the table by the Temple Father, an imposing man with a salt-and-pepper beard and white, gold-trimmed robes. Thalla sat next to them, around the corner of the table. We were waved to seats on the long side of the table across from Thalla.

"Welcome," the Temple Father boomed. "Yon strangers have

opened the veil on a great mystery for us; one we have been pondering for ten years. You have shown us that those who we consider our rivals, and were suspicious of because of their unseemly secretiveness and cruel acts, are indeed our enemy, and probably the enemy of our empire and our people. For this I thank you. It is necessary that we bend our heads together over a common table and see whether this veil can be further pierced, and perhaps completely parted."

"Uh, thank you," Long Harry said.

The Temple Father sat down. "It is nothing. It's our custom to begin talks with an introductory speech, and that was it. I think it's one of the shortest I've made."

"It's surely the shortest I've heard," the Resident Mother said. He glanced at her, but she was smiling sweetly.

"Then you've decided that you do believe us?" The Beak asked, voicing the slight doubt that we all were feeling.

"For sure," the big man boomed. "We tested Sister Thalla's Talent last evening and her empathy level is high enough to have detected evil or malice toward herself or the temple even without her amulet." I looked at Thalla, who was smiling happily across the table, and saw that she was now wearing, on a thin gold chain around her neck, a small, translucent, milk-white stone with internal flecks of jade green, set in a plain gold claw. It looked familiar.

"Is that your Amulet of Rank and Authority?" I asked. "It's very pretty." Thalla was also very pretty, in a thin, white, knee-length robe that clung nicely to all those places girls want robes to cling.

"It's a new one," Thalla said. "I got it last night."

"We all have them," said the Resident Mother. "It's the mark of the order. It serves a much more useful purpose than merely identifying us; it is a focus for the Talent. Mine is also on a neck-chain, while Father Legroot wears his set into a ring." She pulled hers out from under her robes, where it rested neatly in her large, motherly bosom, and Father Legroot displayed his massive, gold pinky ring.

I suddenly remembered where I'd seen one before. "That's very interesting," I said excitedly, "I've seen one of those before. It was...."

"Later," Father Legroot said. "There are many of them around, ours isn't the only order that uses them. I'm sorry to cut you off, but we must get down to the, um, business on the table."

"It's all right," I replied. "Suddenly a lot of things are starting to make sense, but they'll fit into the discussion better later on."

Long Harry gave me a funny look, but didn't say anything.

"The first question is how much do you know about the Temple of Kallo," Father Legroot said.

"Nothing," Long Harry said.

"They speak English," The Beak amended.

"Yes," Father Legroot replied, "They do.

"About ten years ago—that's ten of our years. I don't know how it would correspond to the cycles of your planet around its sun—"

"Neither do we," The Beak said. "You people grasp the implications of new data very rapidly."

"Thank you. About ten of our years ago there was an internal upheaval in the Temple of Kallo, an old temple dating back to before the historic period as does our own, regulating an important Aspect of the Unnamed God Who Has Many Faces: the guise of Kallo, god of battle, god of government, god of the warrior and the official god of herdsmen and transients, god of rocks and metals.

"Of a sudden, new priests took over the positions of authority within the Temple, new policies were instituted, new ways were followed. The Temple started acquiring and using slaves, a practice that is discouraged but not forbidden within the Parsintan Empire and is severely frowned upon by the Established Temples. For a Temple to advocate slavery would be bad enough, but for a Temple to actually use slaves itself was shocking.

"During the traditional yearly meetings of the Council of Established Temples, held on nineday of each new year, the matter has been brought up time after time. The new Archpriests of the Temple of Kallo refuse to discuss it. Last year they threatened not to come again if the slavery question wasn't dropped."

Father Legroot paused while a girl came in with a pitcher of chilled greenwine and six goblets, which she filled and distributed. He took a long drink, carefully dried his lips with a napkin, and continued. "The next question is the language: that which you call English. It was noted that many of the Priests of Kallo spoke this tongue among themselves. We undertook, with the, ah, secret approval of the other Temples, to learn it. Gradually, and with difficulty, we built up a vocabulary. We taught it to select brothers and sisters as the 'sacred language,' with severe instructions not to use it outside the confines of the Temple. Only those in positions of authority were told what it was. I see now that this was a mistake but a lucky one in this case. Not knowing its history, Thalla naturally assumed you were Initiates of Tor when she heard you use it. I will give instructions to remedy this—we won't be so lucky next time. We cannot afford to have the Priests of Kallo know we understand them, it would give away our only edge, and I think we'll need it.

"We must assume now, on the basis of what we have learned from you, that those who took over the Temple of Kallo are men from your planet, and that they are using their position to accomplish some goal, some specific goal, that we do not understand. We must find out what this goal is, possibly the enslavement of our whole country, of our whole world."

"I don't think it's that bad," The Beak said. "No, let me correct that. It might be even worse, but I don't think it's that."

"You have some idea of what it is, then?"

"No, I have no notion. But I think I can tell you what it isn't, on the basis of what would make sense to our people."

"Explain."

"Very well." The Beak paused for a moment, staring down at the table as if to read the secrets hidden in the dark-grained wood. "We come, as you have judged, from a civilization far in advance of your own. Please don't be offended."

"Of course not," Father Legroot snapped, looking offended.

"Well then, these men are criminals on our world, since they are engaged in a criminal act in being here. But they are not known criminals—they haven't been caught at it. Therefore, they probably expect to retire on Earth to a life of wealth and ease on the basis of whatever they're doing here. A life of wealth and ease on Earth, if you have sufficient money, would be preferable to most people to life as a king or emperor here, just as a life of wealth and ease here would be better than being chief of some tribe in your remote past."

Father Legroot nodded. "That makes good sense. Then you think they're doing something here that is worth money to them on this distant planet called Earth. What could that be?"

"I have no idea," The Beak said.

"Perhaps mining some precious metal: gold, silver or copper?"

"No," The Beak said, shaking his head.

Long Harry explained, "the transmatter, the device that brought us here, works on a mass-energy relationship. That is, the heavier the object to be transmitted, the more energy required. Some of the metals, particularly the radioactive, ah, there's no word, the power metals, would be profitable as far as energy costs go, but they can be more easily acquired other places. Actually it's a mass-distance-energy equation, but we haven't traveled far enough into the Galaxy for the distance factor to be important."

"Slaves?" the Resident Mother suggested.

"Slavery is outlawed on Earth," The Beak told her.

"Slaves for use on some other world?"

"That's possible," Long Harry said.

"Possible, but unlikely," The Beak replied. "Our machines are too sophisticated to make. slavery profitable."

"Time, gentlemen," I said, finishing my goblet and refilling it. "This is one of the few times since this mess began that I feel useful. I think I can tell you."

Five heads turned to look at me. "You have an idea?" Father Legroot asked.

"You've been very useful," The Beak told me.

"I think I know what the phony Priests of Kallo are doing on this planet," I said. "Tell me, those stones where do they come from?"

"Stones?" Father Legroot asked, "Oh, the amulets. The *domrim*—amulet gems. They're not very common, although not as rare as some other gemstones. They're found in the sediment of the *Gruz* and *Alpak* Rivers. They wash up from the sea at certain places along the North Coast of Parsint. Very occasionally they're found while mining clay in the Forest of the Dead."

"The what?" Long Harry asked.

"It's called that because formations of rock that look exactly like tree branches or leaves, or sometimes whole trunks, are found there. Our material philosophers have agreed that there's nothing mysterious or supernatural about it, whatever the peasants think. They're just long-dead trees that have turned to stone during the long ages underground."

"We know of such things," The Beak said.

They turned back to me.

"That's it!" I said. "The *domrim* stones are what our renegade Earthmen are after."

"I don't get it," Long Harry said. "Diamonds, maybe...."

"Those stones are much more valuable than diamonds," I told him. "I saw one when I, well, shortly before we left Earth. They called it a telamp."

"Wait a minute," Long Harry said. "Now I know what you're talking about. The telamp, a synthetic gemstone manufactured by the Telamp Corporation, used to amplify psionic powers."

"Amplify, hell," I said. "Nobody even believed in psionic powers before the telamp. They've made it all possible."

The Beak thumped the table with his fist. "You're right! All of a sudden people are practicing telepathy, telekinesis, tele-this and tele-that, all since the telamp. With practice people can use their power without the telamp, but before it was discovered psionic power was too erratic to be believed. About ten percent of those tested have some sort of power. Whole new industries are springing up. All in the past fifteen years. Fifteen years—I'll bet that corresponds to ten years here."

"Right," I said. "And if you change the word 'power' to 'talent' you'll have the whole picture."

"Then they're not synthetic," The Beak said. "No wonder nobody's been able to duplicate them. They're natural, organic gems like pearls or amber."

"That's what I think."

"What do you know of the physical properties of *domrim*?" The Beak asked Father Legroot.

"Physical properties?"

"How hard is it to cut? Does it burn? Things like that."

"The *domrim* is quite hard on the outside and gets softer as you approach the center. It is difficult to ignite, then burns with a smoky flame. Sometimes, after a few moments' burning, it explodes violently, Sometimes it burns straight through. The larger ones usually explode. I've never seen this myself, you understand, they are too rare, but it is so recorded."

"I've never seen telamp," Long Harry said. "They look like this?"

"Exactly," I assured him. "I spent long hours staring at one across a table. It was labeled 'People's Exhibit A'."

"*Domrim* is native only to this world?" Father Legroot asked.

"Apparently so," I replied.

"And that is what these people want?"

"That would be my guess."

"Then why do they need so many slaves?"

Long Harry answered that. "To mine the stone."

"But the only place it can be mined, that we know of, Is in the Forest of the Dead, and few are found there. Besides, the people of the area do the mining. There are no slaves."

"From what you've described," Long Harry told him, "there must be another source. Probably somewhere near the origins of those rivers you mentioned."

"The *Gruz* and the *Alpak*? They are long, mighty rivers. They begin somewhere in the Greel Mountains, to the North.

We will have to search."

"It is a curious coincidence," The Beak said speculatively, rubbing his nose, "that the transmatter slip should have sent us to this planet."

"That's the other thing I think I've figured out," I said. "It wasn't that big a mistake. We were sent here."

"Come now, that machine in the arena wasn't one of ours."

"No, but remember, a slight mistake in coordinates, or in frequencies or whatever it is, can send you to a receiver close to the intended one. A technician at the transmatter must have been in the pay of the Telamp Corporation. If he plugged in a new set of coordinates at the last second, he wouldn't have been able to check them that closely. They must have been fed in by hand instead of using the computer. And I'll bet you the alien machine in the arena, whoever put it there, has an automatic relay that turns it on when something is beamed to it and shuts it off right after. That's how they knew we were somewhere on this planet, too. Their instruments must have showed that we arrived somewhere close."

"It sounds good," The Beak admitted. "I'll bet you're right."

"Oh, Daniel," Thalla said, smiling across the table at me, "you're so clever."

"But why us?" Long Harry asked. "What good could we do them?"

"Not us," I told him. "Me. I'm the only one that's had any contact with a telamp. I must have had some information I didn't realize, or been in a position to figure out something I shouldn't that would be dangerous to them."

"What?" The Beak asked.

"I don't know." My mind whirled over the events of the trial and of Alicia's death. It was, I realized, the first time in weeks that I'd thought of her or my old life. I tried to channel my thoughts. What would I know that no one else would? Everything I knew was public knowledge, the defense attorney, the jury, the judge, whoever had tuned in the trial while it was in progress and whoever wanted a transcript.

Then I saw it. The one thing that only I and the real killer knew. I was not guilty! Everyone else thought I was, and stopped there. No one else was concerned about the real method and motive behind the crime since they thought they knew it. But I knew I hadn't done it, and would keep trying to figure out how and why Alicia was killed. They were afraid I'd succeed, and that would be dangerous to them. How and why was Alicia killed? I still had no idea but I was going to figure it out And I made a resolution: if they thought I was dangerous then, buddy, they ain't seen nothin' yet!

CHAPTER THIRTEEN

It was decided that something must be done about the Priests of Kallo. This was much like the group of mice deciding that something must be done about the cat. No one had any idea of what or how. We lacked sufficient information. Whatever it was, it would have to be done in Parsint, not here.

Father Legroot set about writing up a long report to send under seal to his bosses at the home temple. Thalla was picked as courier and we agreed to go along. We needed them as much as they needed us, as it looked like the Temple of Kallo represented our only way of getting home. We were warned that the two week sea voyage was very dangerous. Long Harry laughed, The Beak smiled. I felt a sinking sensation in my stomach and tried not to show it.

The next ship that could take us was loading now, and would leave in about four days. We met Captain Meeb, master and owner of the good ship *Daxdel-pe-Wizza*, a stern man with long sideburns and little sense of humor, and he said he'd be glad to have us aboard.

"What does the ship's name mean?" I asked him, watching the bustling men stowing bales and crates through the numerous small hatches.

"It be old language," he said. "*Daxdel-pe-Wizza* roughly translates as '*The Craft Which the Sea Gods Will Surely Not Disappoint Too Often.*'"

"I see," I said unhappily. The ship was slender and trim-looking, with three decks and two tall masts, holding one square and one triangular sail. The carved figure of a grinning, toothy sea monster was set into the prow.

Captain Lebipro was very pleased when he found out we were going, as *The Craft Which the Sea Gods Will Surely Not Disappoint Too Often* was the very ship he was leaving on. We were invited to join his farewell dinner party the night before we sailed.

We were very busy the last four days: conferring at the Temple, buying clothes and supplies for the voyage, planning strategy and tactics, drinking greenwine with Captain Lebipro, who seemed to know every tavern and serving-girl in Beloparsus, and fencing. This last was Long Harry's idea. He didn't think there was any point in our wearing swords unless we knew how to use them, and he insisted on our wearing swords.

We must have spent four hours a day at it, and about two hours a day after we boarded the ship. We practiced classical sabre, which both Long Harry and I had done before. I learned mine in my college fencing club. I have no idea where Long Harry picked up his. I was surprised at how much I remembered. My timing was way off, and there was no strength in my wrist, but I know what I was doing. Long Harry was better than I was, and I, to my surprise, was better than Captain Lebipro, who had enthusiastically joined in. Scientific fencing was a new concept on this planet. The Beak wasn't very good except when he got angry, then I wouldn't have liked to tangle with him. What he lacked in technique he made up for in fury.

I remember most of Captain Lebipro's final dinner party, but I don't remember boarding the, ship. The first thing I remember is throwing up over the rail sometime during the night. Then I blanked out again until the middle of the next day. As a slender Colonel of the Guard named Bela kept insisting from his perch on top of a giant barrel of greenwine, it got very drunk out.

That afternoon—the first day out—the sea turned red. It did so very gradually, and at first I wasn't sure it was anything but the reflection of the sun. First a light hint of rosewater red, gradually deepening to port wine red, then darkening to ruby red and thickening to blood red. I stood motionless on the bow, watching as the ship, accompanied by an umbrella of white seabirds, plowed through the glass-smooth blood sea toward the slowly setting sun. It was an almost mystical experience and my mind, ever ready to dredge up primitive mythossymbolism from the racial subconscious, was gathering images and portents of horror below the level of thought and bubbling them up to pop in my conscious brain. I had an awful sense of déjà-vu combined with the certainty of doom. I had sailed this blood-red sea before, and followed it to...a vortex? A smothering? A baking calm and death by madness, thirst and heat? I didn't know but I felt choked and sweaty and tense. Any second I would have to scream.

"It be *pfagorati*," a voice next to me said. "It be always like this during *ifrit*. Underwater reefs, you see. Don't let it bother you."

I surfaced from the currents of my mind and took a deep breath. Captain Meeb was standing by the rail, hands held behind him, staring at the red.

"I, uh, I won't. It's very interesting," I said.

"It be a form of microscopic sea plant. *Skraal* feed on it and the birds feed on *skraal*. Many of the sailors be superstitious about it, and most landsmen be terrified of it. Don't ask me why." He tipped his square, flat cap. "Good eve to you."

"Good eve to you, sir," I said to his broad back as he stolidly stomped away.

The days passed slowly. There was a steady wind and the sails were reassuringly filled out but, to my landsman's eye, it didn't seem as if we were making any headway at all. The water passed around the hull at a good clip, breaking up into tiny bubbles of white foam at the stem, but the horizon stayed endlessly the same. Dull green water stretched out to meet a dirty, white-blue sky at a thin, unchanged line out where the world ended.

We spent a lot of time fencing, to the amusement of the crew watching us slip around the gently weaving deck, and played a constant game of fimbril, a kind of daredevil dominoes.

One night, after about a week, I couldn't sleep so I went up on deck and leaned over the rail, watching the faintly luminous water stream by.

Thalla walked over to me and stood silently for a while, then she spoke. "Hello, Daniel. Are you feeling sick?"

I straightened up. "No, just bored I guess. I couldn't sleep."

She snuggled up next to me. "Me neither. It's nice out here. Kind of cold, but nice."

I put my arm around her to warm her. "Don't you have a cloak? can I get it for you?"

She looked up at me. I couldn't read her expression in the dark. "No thanks. Your arm will do nicely."

"Well, uh," I said, feeling her body pressed against mine, "those stars are very pretty, aren't they? I mean, uh, no clouds or anything."

"Why don't you look at me?" Thalla asked.

"It's dark," I told her. "I couldn't see you too well."

"Try it," she suggested, sliding between me and the rail and looking up at me. "Just get closer, you'll be able to see me very well."

We kissed. Believe me or not, I had no idea we were going to until we did. I suppose I'm dense.

We kissed. After some time, we stopped. Thalla sighed and rested her head on my chest. Her hair tickled my nose. "Well," she said, "If you can't see me, I hope you can feel me."

I stuttered something.

"You *do* like me, don't you?" she asked, lifting her head.

I made an affirmative sound.

"I thought you did. You're not very forward, are you?"

"I didn't think I should say anything," I said, slightly insulted.

"Why not? If you like me, and I like you...."

"Well, you're kind of young, and you're a priestess and you're kind of under my protection, and all...."

"One," she said, tapping her finger on the end of my nose, "I've been old enough for men for several years now. Two, my profession has nothing to do with it. Three, you've been doing such a splendid job of guarding me, I certainly think you deserve some sort of reward. Not that I'm kissing you as a reward. I don't want you to think that. I thought it would be fun, and it is."

"But," I said desperately, "on my world, or at least in my country, girls in religious orders don't, uh, behave...that is—"

"What has my religion got to do with it?"

"Well, you are a priestess."

"That's my job. I serve the Nameless God in his Aspect of Tor, the Messenger God, God of Commerce and the Sea, Overseer of Processes. I do my job well. The customers are satisfied."

"What, exactly, is your job?" I asked.

"The Priestesses of Tor have a wide variety of tasks, which is what makes the life so interesting. Because of my special skills and training I am particularly fit to appear as Official Witness in business dealings, contracts and the like. My command of language makes me useful as an interpreter, and my Talent, Empathy, enables me to witness that all parties did truly negotiate in good faith."

"I see," I said. "But since you represent a religious order, don't your clients expect you to, uh, maintain a high level of decorum and personal conduct?"

"My customers are looking for results. I do my job well. What right have they to care about my personal life?"

I thought about that for a minute, with Thalla's nose against my neck. "Maybe that's it," I said. "Our priests can't guarantee results, so they substitute decorum."

"Kiss me," Thalla demanded.

The rest of the night is none of your business.

* * * * * * *

The next day we sighted the ship.

"Sail in sight!" the lookout called shortly after noon from the watch-basket high atop the main mast. "Three masts, dead astern."

The ship's officers, the off-duty crew and the five passengers went aft to get a look. It was some time before any of us could see anything.

"Sure enough," Captain Meeb said, "there she be." He clapped a brass telescope to his eye and stared through it at the shimmering horizon. "Three masts indeed. Pulling into line. She be headed straight for us."

"What do you think it is?" I asked, straining my eyes to make the dancing motes on the horizon resolve into a ship's masts.

"Warship," Captain Meeb said. "Three-masters be mostly warships."

Long Harry asked, "Friend or foe?"

"Probably not one of ours," the captain answered, capping the telescope and sticking it under his arm. "No reason for it to be in this area." He examined the spread of sail on the *Daxdel-pe-Wizza* with a critical eye. "Let out a notch on the foremast topsail," he yelled, going forward. "Break out the hangers and spinners!"

Within an hour the chasing ship was clearly visible dead astern of us. The crew was kept busy making minute adjustments to the rigging and sails and moving the cargo around below decks to correct the trim of the ship, but we passengers had nothing to do. It proved almost an hypnotic fascination to hang on the stem rail of the ship and watch the distant sails slowly and imperceptibly get larger. The trick was to stick your thumb out in front of your eye until the nail just covered the distant sail and then mark the distance and remove your thumb. Five minutes later you put your thumb back in the same place and see whether the sail has grown larger or smaller under the nail. The only trouble was that none of us could get the same result twice. By nightfall it. became evident that the ship was, indeed, getting larger.

When the captain came back to get a last look in the fading light, I asked him what the chances of the ship's catching us in the dark were.

"Not likely," he said. "If the wind doesn't change, she'll be up with us at about one glass before high noon. Maybe half after one."

"If she's an enemy will we surrender or fight?" I asked.

"If she be an enemy, as she probably be, and she gets that close," the Captain told me, "we'll sink her. We'll blow her out of the water with these new rapid-fire cannon we're mounting. Not a ship in the Urgazteth Navy has as good."

"Well, that's very good news. Then what's everyone looking so worried about?"

"She might be a boarder," Captain Meeb said. "A few of them are, and you can never tell. Then it be a cut and rip fight we're in for, and them as dies might be lucky. The common sailors be mighty superstitious about boarders, but you and me, we're rational folk. Right, lad?"

"I always try to be," I told him. "What's a boarder?"

Captain Meeb slapped me on the back. "That's the attitude. What's a boarder to us? We'll take them as fast as they plink!"

"Plink?"

"Sleep well tonight, son. Good eve to you." He stomped away.

I went in search of Long Harry and found him playing a round of cutthroat fimbril with The Beak. "That ship might be a boarder," I told him. "And it's going to go plink!"

Long Harry put down the tile he was fingering. "Swell," he said. "What does that mean?"

"You tell me," I said. "That's what the captain said, and surely the captain should know."

"Surely," Long Harry agreed, tentatively picking up another tile and examining the layout.

"We ought to make this touch-move, like chess," The Beak groused. "You change your mind more than a pregnant yak."

"Now there," Long Harry said, "is a simile!"

PLINK!

We went out on deck. Nothing seemed to be happening, but then we heard a crashing sound from the foredeck, and the sound of fighting.

PLINK!
PLINK!
PLINK!

The gangways were opening now, and men streamed onto the deck from below. Dressed, half dressed and undressed, each was armed with something and looking for someone to fight.

PLINK!
PLINK!

I looked around for the enemy ship, but it wasn't anywhere in sight. Even in the dark I would have been able to make out its outline if it was within a hundred yards of us.

PLINK!

A man appeared on the deck in front of us. I mean *appeared*, not darted or dropped. One instant there was empty space, the next there was this man. He was dressed all in black in some sort of form-fitting material; even his head was hooded except for an oval uncovering eyes, nose, and mouth. The long, curved blade in his hand was as dark as the night he came out of, and for a second I fancied I could see stars shining through it.

With his mouth open in silent scream, he attacked, the only sound his feet padding across the deck. Long Harry, in one wide motion, drew his sword and parried the downward sweep of the blackened blade.

PLINK! PLINK!
PLINK!

I pulled my own sword as another silent swordsman pinged into existence behind us. Warned by the *PLINK!* I was ready for him when he attacked with silent fury. Then there were three of them against us and Long Harry and I fought back-to-back. I fenced steadily against one, while Long Harry, with broad sweeps of his blade, kept the other two away.

Silent and furious the plinker may have been, but his hacking attack was no match for science. The fencing practice paid off in short order. Parry, parry, lunge, and I was under his guard with a solid thrust to the body. With a look of surprise, he fell as quietly as he had fought.

I turned to help Long Harry with his two, but he had managed well without me. The two were now one and that one was backing away steadily as he fought off Long Harry's flashing attack. With a final thrust, his opponent dropped his sword and dived over the rail into the night sea. We heard the splash when he hit, but couldn't even make out the water when we peered over the side.

The Beak had found a six-foot staff somewhere, and was using it to hold off four of our mysterious adversaries. With his back to the ladder which led to the pilot house containing the ship's wheel, he whacked and thrust about him with a steady rhythm, keeping his opponents from their objective. We ran to his side and, with the aid of a cutlass-wielding sailor, broke up the attack and dispatched the attackers.

The deck was now clotted with knots of sailors and black-clad plinkers. Now that any initial surprise to be gained by silence was gone, our enemy in black was yelling battle curses as loudly as the ship's company. The din of steel on steel and human screams sounded over the ship. The only light came from the glow of ship's lanterns shining through an occasional opened batch or porthole. The whole scene, combined of shifting, patchwork elements of men weaving to and fro in the drunkenness of battle; stumbling, slipping, guarding, thrusting, slashing, dodging, falling, bleeding, and over all screaming the battlemad screams of fear and challenge that are one step beyond reason, is imprinted in my brain. It is said that at no'time are we so truly alive as when threatened by immediate death, and in this way, at this time, it's true. Complete sense memories of this fight-crazed few minutes; the sights and sounds, the sea-smell, the chill breeze, the sway of the deck, the taste in my mouth and the heat-throb of muscles and sinews working on emergency reserve, are preserved in a tape loop of vivid memory.

I joined the melee in a battle-passion whetted by my first successful sword-fight and turned on by the cries of those around me. My hands and feet were moved by long forgotten instinct, reacting to the needs of mortal combat, while somewhere deep inside my head I sat and watched and marveled and was afraid.

I battled two men and was losing step by step until The Beak joined my side and we stood and then advanced, driving them back to the mainmast, where they broke and dodged away rather than getting trapped against its rounded side. I thought this most unsporting of them, considering all the work we'd put into backing them there. We didn't chase but looked for new targets. I think The Beak was as infected as I by the roar of fighting around us.

Captain Meeb stood on a hatch and shouted commands above the din. His voice carried across the ship, and he formed an ordered battle line of sailors out of the screaming mob.

The enemy's only hope of a clean-cut victory had been in catching us off guard, and this was gone. They gathered in several tight groups and, while half held off our men, the others cut all the rigging they could reach. The lower sail on the square-rigged foremast fell with a series of short cracks and a final, sodden crash, but this was the last damage they could do. Too hard pressed to remain, the little black-clad groups mounted the rail and dived into the inky sea below.

The blood fury passed, and I stood where I was, fist clenched around a lead-weight sword, arm raised to slash the night air. My arm dropped and I sank to the deck exhausted and shaking, my lungs sobbing for air. My fingers, white-knuckled, would not release the sword and I had to pry them apart with my other hand.

"Topmen!" the Captain bellowed, "reeve the foresail lines and get her set! They're trying to make us lose enough headway to overhaul us in the night and board by force. We won this one, boys! We won't let 'em try again!"

Someone cheered and the whole crew took it up until the sound was louder than the just passed battle din. I don't know where they got the air. I was having enough trouble breathing.

"Get on!" the captain yelled when the cheers had died. "Forward berth man the guns. I want 'em loaded and run out and the slow match passed, but that be all. Any man that fires without command will answer! Mid berth check the ship for damage and for skulking boarder. Aft berth assemble the dead and wounded and help the surgeon's crew. Get on!"

When I could stand I helped assemble bodies on the deck. We lined them up in two neat rows. I was glad of the dark. I didn't want to see the faces. Long Harry helped. The Beak and Thalla went to aid the ship's surgeon with the wounded. Thalla had been asleep with the fighting started, and had come on deck to see what all the noise was about. She had watched the whole thing from her doorway, clutching a wooden spike, and at one point had darted forward long enough to clobber a boarder who seemed to be getting the better of the sailor he attacked. I didn't know whether to be proud or horrified.

Captain Meeb came down to inspect the bodies. Fourteen dead of ours and nineteen that we could find of our opponents'. "Not bad," he said. "We gave them better than we got. I doubt me if they'll try that again. These be fine men, fine men. It be a shame!"

The black garb of the boarders was a skintight suit of a gummy rubber outer layer over sewn canvas, a sort of primitive wet-suit. Each man also wore a canvas web belt with a sewn slit to hold a naked sword.

"How did they get aboard?" I asked.

"You didn't see?" the Captain asked.

"I saw something, but I'm not sure what," I told him. "They

sort of appeared out of the air."

Captain Meeb said, "That's just what. They be boarders, projected through the night void by Talent and trained to fight the instant they plink aboard. They fight to cripple the ship and engage the crew long enough for their ship to come alongside and capture us. They're nothing supernatural, just applied magic."

"I understand," I said.

The Captain sighed and rubbed his hands along the sides of his neck. "Well, I guess I'd better arrange for the sea-death reading. There be no point to put it off. The men will take it better with the taste of victory still fresh in their mouths."

"What about these?" Long Harry asked, indicating the rubber-clad bodies of our recent foe.

"They'll be—here, see it for yourself!" The captain pointed and, as we watched, the black-suited corpses vanished one by one with a series of faint clapping sounds to mark their passing.

"What—" I said.

"The Talent sends them here for but a time," the Captain said. "And then, alive or dead, they make the journey back."

Call it scientific, or magic, or Talent, any name you like, it was an eerie sight, those still black forms passing from existence with just a rush of air to tell where they had been.

CHAPTER FOURTEEN

"It can be done," Beolakak, the high priest, decided. "It shall be done!"

We had landed in Parsint and found that we were expected, the temple in Beloparsus had sent word of our coming by fast pigeon, but no more than that; the cargo capacity of a pigeon was limited. A two-pimpady carriage was waiting at the pier to take us directly to the Temple and a round of iteration, explanation, discussion and decision.

Beolakak believed in immediate, directed action. *Delenda est Carthago*. The false priests of Kallo must be eliminated. We agreed with him, the only problem was how.

Their one unbeatable asset was not the Earth weapons they might already have, but their pipeline, the transmatter. The odds were great that they had only one terminal. The required energy was enormous, but we didn't have any idea where it was.

"Couldn't you," I asked, thinking of the shipboard battle, "send someone as a scout using the Talent? Or doesn't it go far enough?"

"It goes as far as we have ever ranged it," an elderly priestess told me. "But we have to know the place we're sending to."

The conversation at the great round conference table stopped while everyone mulled this over.

"Not—quite!" Beolakak said. He stood up, revealing a tall beard that made his huge head seem too heavy to be held up by a human neck. "It can be done. It shall be done!"

"How?" someone asked.

He turned and whispered to a green-robed acolyte, who raced from the room. "Yon shall see," he said, nodding to us. "We must be quick, we must be decisive, and we must be victorious. We shall send our spy to locate this *machine*"—he spat the word—"and we shall prepare to act the instant it is found. Those who foster slavery, murder, and piracy, those who would divide us to control, those visitors who do evil on two worlds, they must be stopped! They shall be stopped! I pledge it."

The acolyte returned with a hunk of milk-white rock, flecked with green, and handed it to Beolakak. He raised it in his hand. "Here is our tool," he said, and dropped it to the table, where it crashed and rolled out to the middle.

"*Domrim!*" a priestess identified. "But how? We all have our own...." She fingered the smooth stone on her necklace.

"This stone is newly mined," Beolakak said. "Two days ago a slave sought sanctuary in our Temple. He carried this. Look at it."

The priestess examined the rock. She ran her fingers over it gently, as if handling a newborn child, then lifted it and held it to the light. "Beautiful! But the lines—this stone is twinned from some much larger rock. Yes, here's the node." She lowered her hands and kept staring at the stone, which hung unsupported above the table. Then she leaned back, stroking the stone set in her necklace, and its cousin sank slowly to the table.

The stone was passed among the experts, and they all agreed. It was suspended twice more, and once flipped from one side of the table to the other, but some of these Followers of Tor just stared into its depths and smiled. There was a lot of Talent around the table.

"Then we're all agreed?" Boelakak asked. "Good! Let us prepare. Select the ring and the follower and make ready."

"It should be one of them," the old priestess said. "Our friends from Earth. They will know best what they see and how to search for what we seek."

"I will ask it of them," Boelakak said. "My friends, would you undertake this mission for us? You may refuse. You have been through much already."

"You lost us there somewhere," Long Harry said. "What do you want us to do?"

"I do apologize," the High Priest said. "Of course, you could not follow.... This stone that we have here is a small, natural bud of a much larger gem. The *domrim* are never cut, so it is rare to have such a sister-stone. The larger one, we must assume, is in the possession of the Priests of Kallo. If that is so we have the means to put a spy inside their camp. With a ring of Talent focused on the smaller stone, we can send a man to where the larger rests. This, of course, is dangerous. If it rests around the neck of some priest, our spy would be caught and tortured, if not killed."

"But," The Beak said, "if we're right and they're sending these stones back to Earth, it will probably be sitting somewhere awaiting shipment."

"Correct," Beolakak said. "We ask one of you to go as you can identify the machine we seek more easily than we. Once it is found, then we can puzzle out what to do."

"Fine by me," Long Harry said.

"Also," The Beak agreed. "We have an interest. Those men are trying to kill us."

"It's me they're trying to kill," I insisted. "I got you into this. It's my job to get you out."

"We'll draw straws," Long Harry suggested.

"Thank you," the High Priest said. "We shall prepare."

The adventure was scheduled for the next morning. We drew straws that evening in our apartment (we had been assigned a suite of rooms in the temple, separate bedrooms and baths, living room, dining room, entrance room and a couple without assigned functions). Thalla was with us, looking happy. The first try ended in an argument, but on the second I clearly won.

"May the god of chance ride on your shoulder," Thalla said. "I will be in the ring tomorrow, since my knowledge of you and my Empathy will help the rapport."

"That's good," I said. "I'll feel better with you there."

"You know what you're looking for?" Long Harry asked.

"Sure," I said. "A transmatter room."

"Or a power source," he, said. "Remember, those things take an awful lot of power when they transmit."

"Say," I said. "I just had a thought—are we sure we want to do this?"

"You don't want to go?" Long Harry asked. "I'll go...."

"It's not that at all," I replied. "I want to get my hands on a couple of these bastards. It's just that, if we're right, and they have only one transmatter on the planet, we're cutting ourselves off if we destroy it. Maybe we should try to capture it whole."

"You want to go back to Earth?" Long Harry asked. "Forget it. You'd just end up back where we started and the place they send you won't be as good as right here. I guarantee it."

"But I'm not guilty," I said. "I didn't, ah, do what they accused me of, and I think I can prove it now."

"To whom?" The Beak asked. "A jury of your peers, twelve good men and true, said you did. The state hates to be wrong."

"Besides, relax!" Long Harry said. "There's got to be a transmatter planted on some airless planet in the system by the wave ship. If for some reason we decide to, I'm sure we can find a way to get to it. There's also the alien transmatter in the arena. We should be able to figure out how to use it."

"I thought you had some urgent business back on Earth?" I asked The Beak. "I seem to remember you mentioning it once or twice."

The Beak nodded, looking grey and old, and I was sorry I'd asked him. "I've been thinking it over. It's been preying on my mind. The kid'll be better off without me. I've been slow realizing it, and slower admitting it even to myself. I'll say no more about it."

And he didn't. We went to bed early and, to my surprise, I fell asleep almost immediately.

I awoke to Thalla's shaking in the morning. "Come on," she said. "Ablute and come on. We must get going, they'll be waiting for us."

I followed instructions and staggered down the hall with Thalla. It always takes me a while to start functioning after I wake up. We entered a plain, large room with a marble floor. A group of men and women were already there, talking softly and drinking tea. Someone shoved a mug in my hand and I sipped it gratefully. My blood started flowing, my brain starting turning over and the film in front of my eyes slowly dissolved.

High Priest Beolakak came in and gulped down a mug of tea. "Good morning," I said.

He nodded. "Come," he said. "We'll get you dressed." He took me over to a side room. "Strip down to your undergarments and put this on."

A two-piece version of the rubber suit, this one in brown, was hanging up on pins. "Sure," I said, starting to comply. "Why?"

He helped me pull the thing over my legs and arms. It fitted like an elastic bandage. "It will protect you from the cold and lack of pressure when you make the trip."

"I thought it would be instantaneous," I said.

"It takes a finite length of time, like the sound of clap."

"How do I get back?" I asked, sticking my fingers into the pair of thin rubber gloves. "Some sort of signal or do you pull me back when you think I'm done?"

"The trip is temporary in nature. You will return of yourself with nothing from us. We will send you as strongly as possible and you will return before the day is out. Few could achieve this length of time."

We returned to the room and made ready. The group formed a large circle, sitting cross-legged on the floor. I don't know what I expected, but it was nothing this simple. I stood in the circle facing Thalla (my choice) and the stone rested a few feet away from me. Some of the group stared fixedly at the stone, some stared at me, a few closed their eyes and rocked gently back and forth.

PLINK!

I was floating to all points to which the Universe had not yet expanded. My body took in all infinity except that one bright spot. There was no time.

"THIS PIECE IS NOT OF OUR GAME!"

"THEN DO NOT PLAY IT. PROCEED."

Those voices/thoughts again. "Who are you?" I screamed, soundlessly.

"SHODDY WORKMANSHIP. I SHALL SPEAK TO THE REFEREE."

I was standing in a room, shivering, with no idea how long I'd been there or how I had arrived. Then my mind clicked back.

I looked around, rubbing my arms to warm them and thinking that this form of travel would never get popular. The room was dully lit by a row of filthy windows along one wall, and was full of packages and crates of all sizes. A storage-room or warehouse. Where did I go from there?

The first thing was to find out where I was. I went over to a window and tried to peer out through the thick layer of grime, but I couldn't see anything. I found a hunk of straw on the floor and rubbed it against one pane to clear a space to look through.

I was in New York!

I shook my head and stared through the glass again. There was no mistaking the skyline. Unless I was having delusions, I was on a high floor in a downtown office building.

I thought about that for a minute. At first it didn't make sense, then it came to me. The domrim stone must have been shipped through, and this was the receiving end. The Talent was a lot stronger than I had supposed.

What next? My first impulse was to sit there until I snapped back and explain the mistake. They could try again some other way.

Then I had an idea. The traffic could be stopped just as easily by the authorities at this end, once they knew what was going on. I had to go find an authority quickly and tell him enough to get an investigation started.

What authority? The problem with thinking for yourself is that you have to ask the questions as well as answer them., Thinking for someone else is always easier. The authority that regulated the problem, obviously.

Yes, that's fine, but; what is the problem? I sat down to think it out. The problem, I decided, was to get a group of Earthmen off an interdicted planet. That defined my authority for me: the Alien Culture Regulatory Committee, the same group Senator Ben Isaak von Turner had been chairman of before he, and Alicia, died.

Aha! Now everything slid neatly into place. I had all the details. Of course, I couldn't prove anything but a professional investigation would be able to turn up supportive evidence.

I had. to move fast. I found the door to the hall, which opened without trouble from the inside, and peered out. There was nobody in sight. I slipped out, closing the door behind me, and walked as silently as I could manage down the hall looking for the elevators.

Footsteps!. I flattened against the door as a guard turned the corner and started toward me. It took him two steps to notice me, and he stopped short. "Hey! What're you doing...." One leap and I was on him. A stiff hand to the solar plexus and an uppercut to the chin and he was down.

I started to strip off my rubber suit, then remembered I'd need it to get back. I searched the guard's pockets for a pen knife, found one on his key chain, and carefully cut the hood off the rubber suit low around the neck. Then I removed the guard's uniform and put it on. It was tight in the shoulders and very loose around the waist, even over the rubber suit. Soft living. I tightened the pistol belt up to the last notch. There wasn't any place I could put the guard, so I left him there and strode over to the bank of elevators.

I jabbed my finger at the down button but it wouldn't light up. *Oh fine*, I thought. *Sunday or Saint Crispin's Day or something; I'll have to walk down.* Then I realized what it was. The contact plate worked by induction, and I was wearing rubber gloves. I tried to slide one off, but the thing had tightened on like new skin. So I bent down and touched the switch with the tip of my nose.

The elevator was big and luxurious, with soft carpeting, indirect lighting and insipid music. It stopped at every other floor, opened the door six inches low, and seemed to be mumbling something.

The ground floor lobby was crowded with people as I left the elevator and started toward the street. I'm sure that not all of them could have stopped what they were doing and turned to stare at me. It just felt that way. I hailed a cab from the sidewalk and, using the guard's identab, had it take me to the nearest commuter shuttle station.

The station was large and comfortably anonymous, but the guard's uniform was too conspicuous and made me feel uneasy. I couldn't afford to be stopped before I got where I was going. There wasn't enough time.

I had just missed the train to Washington and had to wait ten minutes for the next. I went into the men's room and over to the corner with a row of private booths containing showers and tiny dressing rooms. The tabs showed that two of them were occupied, so I waited, pretending to shine my shoes or comb my hair whenever anyone walked by.

The first man to come out of a booth was short and fat and gave me a startled look as he went by. I let him go. The second door opened and a man about my height in a conservative tunic carrying an overnight case stepped out. I pushed against him, catching the door before it closed, and shoved him back inside.

"What the—listen buddy," he snarled, "you've got the wrong guy, I'm not that type."

I stepped inside the booth and closed the door. We were completely cut off.

"I warned you," the man said, balling his hands into fists. He had heavy muscles under those well-cut sleeves. He swung a savage right to my head, followed with a short, left chop that would land right where my midsection would be when I ducked the first blow.

I sidestepped his right, grabbing his elbow and pulling it around so his fist went into the steel door. He bellowed and turned back, to face the guard's pistol pointed square at his nose.

"Take your clothes off," I said.

*   *   *   *   *   *   *

The half-hour trip to Washington was smooth and uneventful. I still had the rubber suit on under my borrowed clothes, but I had managed to remove the gloves and shove them into my pockets. I took two newspapers with me and spent the time reading both from masthead to classified. The gentleman who shared my compartment kept his nose buried in a tablet reader for the whole trip and we happily ignored each other.

Right before we arrived I extracted a needed bit of information from him. "Say," I said, staring myopically at an article in the gardening section of the paper, "sorry to bother you, but do you happen to know who is the present chairman of the, ah, Alien Culture Regulatory Committee?"

"What's that?"

"Never mind, sorry I bothered you."

"No trouble. I never follow any of that stuff. Always meant to take up a hobby, but never had the time—you know how it is. Wait a second." He tapped a taradiddle on the screen of his reader. "Here it is: fellow named Glister, Senator Eugene Gerard Glister. Glad to help." He went back to his reader.

The Washington telephone book listed Senator Glister's offices as being in the Old New Senate Office Building. I debated calling first, but decided it would either be a waste of time or actually dangerous. I wanted to be able to tell him the whole story before he just had me carted off as a nutty escaped convict. If I alerted him over the phone he just might have a couple of bluecoats pick me up in his office.

I walked from the station to the Old New Senate Office Building. The smog was really getting bad; I could see the wall of yellow-green air pressing against the sides of the dome. Pollution Control kept saying. that in another five or ten years they'd have the problem licked, but every month it got worse. They kept breeding Hardy Vegetation and trying to plant it outside the domes, but the smog killed it; and every year the oxygen level in the natural atmosphere dropped lower. You could still go outside without a mask for up to half an hour after a heavy rain, but nobody did any more; at least, not for pleasure.

Senator Glister's office was listed as B1441-9. I got in the elevator and discovered that the B listing meant that it was 14 floors underground. I pressed the button and went down.

The door to B1441 said *SENATOR GLISTER reception* and the rest of the doors in the row said *private*. I tried all the *private*s first and found them locked, so I went in *reception*.

"Yes?" the receptionist lilted, a constituent smile on her face.

"I'd like to see the senator," I told her. "It's important and urgent."

"Have you an appointment?" she asked.

"No."

"If you'll tell me the nature of your business I'll see whether I can make an appointment for you."

"I have to see the senator now," I told her. "I have information about a criminal enterprise on an interdicted planet, and if I don't get to see him now I won't be able to see him at all."

The girl stared at me and I looked back, projecting earnestness and sincerity as hard as I could.

"Could I have your name, please?" she asked.

I sighed. At least she was going to consult higher authority. "Godfrey," I told her. "Daniel Godfrey."

She pushed a button on her desk and a skinny man popped through a rear door like he was on springs. "I'm going in back for a minute," she told him. "Watch the office." What she meant was watch me, and he did. She was in back for about ten minutes. "You're in luck, Mister Godfrey," she told me when she came out. "The Senator's here today, and he'd like to see you. Sam, please take this gentleman back to the Senator's office."

Senator Glister was fat and jovial. He pumped my hand and waved me to a chair. "You have information for me, I believe?" he said. "It's public-spirited citizens like yourself that our government depends on." He sat down and folded his hands over his belly. "Well?"

I told all I knew, or had deduced, about the Telamp Corporation and the Priests of Kallo. I wasn't sure where to begin, but once I started the information organized itself and flowed in a smooth stream of words. He didn't interrupt at all, but sat there staring intently at me and steadily eating cookies from a box on the desk.

"That's quite a serious charge you're making, and against one of our most influential corporations," he said after I ran down. "And you say you were being transported for murder when this accident happened and you landed in this interdicted world?"

"That's part of it," I said. "It was no accident, and I didn't commit murder. They killed Senator Turner and sent someone into his office to steal the report he was preparing by using one of these Telamp stones. I guess their agent didn't expect to find Alicia Grundel there, and he killed her to keep her quiet."

"Wouldn't a heatgram have shown that someone else was there?"

"Not if he was wearing a rubber suit and was ice cold from the trip—that's one of the side effects."

"A rubber suit?"

"With gloves like this." I pulled one out of my pocket and slapped it on his desk. He jumped back like it was a live scorpion.

"Hum, you startled me. Hum." He pushed a switch. "I'll check your story. You realize that you'll have to go back to prison until it's checked out?"

"I won't be there long," I said.

"I'm sure that if you're telling me the truth we can have you out of there in no time," he assured me.

I was about to explain that that wasn't what I'd meant, when two uniformed guards popped through the door. Everyone in this place seemed to be on springs.

"Take this gentleman to the guards at Lowenstahl Hightower," Senator Glister told them. "I'll call them up and tell them to expect him." He shook hands with me again. "Sorry about this; a mere formality."

Two guards in dull pink uniforms were waiting for us at the entrance to Lowenstahl Hightower, a squat building across the river from the Roosevelt Monument. "Mister Godfrey?" the taller one asked.

I acknowledged the fact.

"Come with us," he said.

Again an elevator took me down, this time for what seemed a considerable distance. We came out into a small, cage-like room, with two guards standing before a barred door. They opened it for us with no formality, and we went through into the large room beyond.

"Say!" I said, looking around. "What is this?"

"A transmatter portal," the smaller guard said nastily. "I'm sure you've seen one before."

"Now look," I said. "You can't just—"

"Shut up," the small one said, pulling a big gun out and waving it around in the general direction of my face. "Don't cause any trouble and you won't get any. Climb up onto the platform."

I climbed. It came to me that I had picked the wrong senator to tell my story to. A couple of plain-clothes technicians muttered figures back and forth to each other, and one of them hit a switch.

I dropped through hot water and came out dry, and the room outside had changed. Everything was undecorated white marble: floor, walls, and high ceiling, except for a large pair of black double doors. It looked like the men's room in an old time movie theater. Three men in flowing robes and high, ornate headdresses were standing waiting for me. One of them had a submachine gun cradled under his arm.

"Welcome," the one in the highest headdress said in English, "we've been expecting you." He gestured to the unarmed third, who flipped a row of switches on the transmatter desk-console in the middle of the room to turn all the operating lights back to green. They must have had a heavy schedule.

"Thank you," I said. "It's nice to be needed."

"Join us," the priest said. "We have a few questions we'd like to ask you." They took me off, the platform and tied my hands behind my back. Then we went in procession, with me in the middle, through the black doors, across a second room littered with open and closed packing crates, and up a flight of stone steps. It was like a scene from a Mayan sacrifice, with me playing the central role.

The march ended in a small, wood-paneled room with a bench and a couple of chairs. I got the bench. The headdress with the submachine gun stood by the door, smiling like a toothpaste ad.

"A few questions," my inquisitor repeated, breathing sweet-scented evil info my face. "Start with two to see how cooperative you are without persuasion. How many people did you tell your story to, and where is your transmatter machine? Also, where are your comrades?"

"That's three," I told him. "count it up on your fingers."

He slapped me, swinging his hand wide from the shoulder. I almost slid off the bench, but righted myself. My face stung, and tears welled into my eyes. I shook me head to clear my eyes. "That hurt," I said. "You've made your point."

He slapped me again, backhand. I fell off the bench and was roughly pulled back onto it. My face was stinging like I'd run into a swarm of bees, and I could feel something warm and sticky run down my cheek. I saw that his fingers were knobbed with heavy, jeweled rings. He must have cut my cheek open badly with that backhanded swipe.

I could feel the pulse at my temple throbbing heavily, and a bank of tension settled across my chest like a physical thing. I was boiling angry; I wanted to kill him and rip apart everything in sight. Most people, when they're put in a helpless position and faced with physical pain, break down quickly and will say or do anything to get out. A small minority get so angry that their resistance toughens. I am, unfortunately, of that sort. I would have died before telling him my right name. Understand, I'm a physical and mental coward; if he'd if he'd tried fear, if he'd just *threatened* to beat me, if he'd done any of a hundred other things, he'd have me. But the feeling of helplessness and pain set off a rage so deep I couldn't do anything but taunt him. And it hurt me a lot worse than it hurt him.

"You will answer my questions," he said, his eyes closed down to black points. "Where is your transmatter?"

"Please!" I said. "No personal questions."

Slap!

"Where are your comrades?"

"Behind you."

He almost looked, then turned back to me and slugged me off the bench.

"What can you hope to gain by this?" he asked me when I was reseated. "You can see that you're going to have to tell me what I ask."

"I'm a masochist," I said, "and if I tell you, you'll stop hitting me."

He stood up, his fists clenched, and slowly turned red in the face. "Enough!" he said. "I have not time for this. Take him upcountry and work on him. When you have the answers, get rid of him!" he stalked out of the room, twitching the skirts of his robe.

I was taken down a long corridor with thick wood-beam ceilings decorated with carved fish heads, and down a wooden stairway. After two turns it became a flight of stone steps leading on to an ill-lit wharf. The stones of the wharf were well-worn, and the whole had an odor of fishy decay. Along the front, tied up to a row of ancient, sea-creature-carved posts, a few small boats were rocking gently, surrounded by slime-covered flotsam.

I was folded at gunpoint into a small chest, which was closed and locked, and then carried, kicked, shoved and dropped into one of the boats.

I ached all over: my face burned from the savage slaps, my arms and shoulders were sore and twisted, and my wrists and forearms were numb from the tight ropes. I tried to relax all my muscles, and found that I couldn't move: I was clamped into a doubled-over position in the small chest. I was not comfortable.

I was bitter cold and gasping for air, spinning into the maelstrom center of my soul. And then, numb, I fell through into white-blinding vacuum. It lasted forever. It lasted no time at all. I landed and collapsed on a marble floor.

CHAPTER FIFTEEN

They peeled off the rubber suit and put a mattress under me and wrapped blankets around me and fed me hot tea. They rubbed my wrists where they had been bound—both binding ropes and stolen oversuit stayed behind when I returned—and applied cool salves. With amazing self-control, they waited until I had finished the first cup of tea before asking any questions.

I told the assemblage all the details I could think of. It reminded me of a ninth-grade recital of "My Trip." The next speech, I remembered, would be "What Thanksgiving Means to Me."

"Well, well, well," Beolakak said enthusiastically. "Well, well. They must think you're still in that trunk. There's no time to lose—we attack tonight!"

"Can you find the place?" I asked him. "I didn't get too much chance to look for identifying characteristics."

"Nonetheless I recognize it from your description. You were in the Sea-Lodge Temple on the Street of the Odor of Lamentable Decay, by the river."

"Good," I said. "I'm glad the whole experience wasn't wasted. Get me some clothes, and let's go!"

"You're not in very good condition to lead a war-party," the Beak insisted. "Don't hog all the glory."

"You need me," I told Beolakak. "I know where the room is; I can lead you right to it. Besides, I want to get my hands on that guy with the big hat."

The high priest nodded. "Come along, then, if you think

you're up to it. I have leather and steel for all of you. Get ready quickly."

The minions of good were waiting for us when we came downstairs.

"I lead," Boelakak said. "Nothing else is permissible." He was very firm about it.

The force, numbering about fifty, alternated between swordsmen and crossbowmen. As we trotted in double-file down to the waiting boats, I couldn't help remembering the submachine gun and wondering what I was doing there.

We split up among three flat-bottom barges and stood, sat or squatted on the deck, trying to keep out of the way of the rowers. Our barge took the lead, poling out into the current and settling down for the steady row upstream.

Five men gathered around Beolakak in front of the barge. They took off their cloaks, and I could see that they were wearing rubber suits like the one I had just gotten out of.

"What're they going to do?" I asked Long Harry, who was squatting alongside me, honing the edge of his sword on a piece of leather.

"They go in first," he told me. "We've got two priests with the Talent on board, and they're going to project those men onto the dock. Just to give us a little edge."

"You don't have to convince me," I said "I'm for any little edge we can manage. I'm not sure Beolakak really understood what I told him about the power of a machine gun."

"Remember," Long Harry said, "The power of prayer. And you may pause to reflect that it's better to be prayed for than preyed on." He gave a satisfied nod

"I don't understand," I said.

"Pretend you do; it can't hurt."

We rowed on. Beolakak appointed six men to go with me. We were to head straight for the transmatter, regardless of what was happening around us, and destroy it.

"There!" Beolakak said, pointing to the shore with his chin. "That's the river dock of the Temple."

"Why are we going past it?" I asked.

"We'll get upstream of it, so we can pull in faster and more easily." He watched the river and the shoreline critically, humming a peaceful tune between his clenched teeth.

"Now!"

The five rubber-clad men disappeared from the deck, and the barges swung ponderously around and headed for the dock.

We came in solidly, ramming into the side of one of the small boats and crashing into the pilings. The rowers leapt out and secured the barge, and we all scrambled onto the dock. Our advance scouts were standing there grinning, on an otherwise deserted platform. "Was the dock empty?" Beolakak demanded in a hoarse whisper.

"Wasn't," one of them answered. "Is now."

We went as quietly as possible up the stairs and spread out, heading in different directions through the building. My group and I raced down the corridor toward the second staircase. Behind us came the first sound of opposition: a high scream of rage, cut off sharply in mid-blast. As we reached the stairway a gong sounded, tolling slowly and steadily with a deep note that reverberated throughout the building.

One of the crossbowmen tapped me on the shoulder. "I believe they know we're here," he murmured.

"Downstairs, quickly," I said. We clattered down the stairs, now concentrating on speed and giving up any attempt at silence.

A startled priest was backing down the stairs as I rounded the landing, and was tugging at a metal object clipped to his waist inside the flowing robe. Gun or knife? No time or interest in finding out; I swung around, launching myself off the banister feet-first and heels together. I hit somewhere around mid-chest, and we rolled and tumbled down the stairs together. When we hit bottom, I was the only one to get up. My knees hurt, but such is the price of glory.

I waited for my crew to catch up, and then peered cautiously around the door frame. There was no one in sight, which suited me fine. We tiptoed cautiously out into the large storage-room which led to the transmatter chamber. "Spread out," I whispered, and started toward the large, black double doors.

The door started opening, and then slammed closed as whoever was behind it saw us. "Come on!" I yelled, breaking into a run.

The door banged open, and a white-robed figure dived out, somersaulting toward the protection of a large crate, firing a machine gun wildly in our direction as he rolled. The explosive yammering of detonating cartridges blotted out all other sound, painfully echoing across the marble walls. Then it stopped.

White-robe slid the last few feet, his head banging sharply against the side of the crate and the machine gun spinning from his hands. A thick, black quarrel was half buried in the ornate high collar of the robe, and a surprised and vaguely displeased expression was set on his face.

"Good shot!" I said. "come on now, let's—" My leg buckled under me, and I sat down. Feeling foolish, I tried to stand up, but the leg wouldn't work. I looked down. An ever-widening circle of red was spreading from a neat, small hole in my thigh.

"You're hurt!" one of the bowmen noticed.

"I don't feel a thing," I said. "But I don't think I can walk. Help me in there so I can get at that machine." Two bowmen hit the door low and dived into the room on their bellies, crossbows ready. A small, unhappy-looking man stood in the center of the room, hands held well above his head. They quickly scouted the rest of the room, but he was alone.

They brought back the swivel chair from behind the console desk and helped me into it, then wheeled me over to the control panel. There was a loud, insistent ringing in my head and things were starting to spin around, but I concentrated long enough to find the power and calibration boards. I unsnapped the inspection hinges and pulled the units out on their rollers. "These two," I said. "Break 'em up. Then work on the rest. Pull that switch there first, and you won't get hurt." The men swarmed around the console, and I dropped swiftly into unconsciousness amid the sound of cracking plastic and snapping metal.

CHAPTER SIXTEEN

As a wise and aging bull terrier of my acquaintance once said, never corner a rat. Give him a bolt hole he can escape through and then rip him up when he tries. The Priests of Kallo/renegade Earthmen/Telamp Corporation would never have given up the profitable domrim thievery without a fight. So they retreated to their bolt-hole—Earth—to prepare the invasion. Deprived of the only transmatter on the planet that they knew of, they took a planetary rocket they had hidden in the mountains to Krabletog, the fifth planet in the system, where the weave ships had hidden the original contact transmatter. There, safely out of our reach, they returned to Earth.

They didn't realize, as I hadn't, the power of *domrim*-aided Talent.

I was in bed for five days. The bullet hadn't hit anything important, and was easily removed, but I had lost a lot of blood. On the sixth day I made it to a wheelchair, and the Earthmen took off, leaving a bungle of baffled underpriests, slaves and equipment.

A circle of Talented telepaths and clairvoyants followed the ship from the moment of takeoff, even giving us a transcript of a good bit of the mostly unprintable dialogue of the furious high priest. When the ship landed on Krabletog a joint sense-impression of the spot was made by the circle.

The Beak spent four days fashioning a workable vacuum suit, which, given the available technology, looked something like a giant carrot with arms. After careful instruction, a volunteer donned the suit and stepped into the circle. He appeared within five yards of the transmatter, hopped over to it, and disconnected its power source and remote control.

The gate was closed from this side until and unless we decide to reopen it.

We're going to be busy for some time examining the equipment that our friends left behind and seeing what can best be used here. In some cases, like refining fuel for the helicopters, it's a matter of making the tools to make the tools. In some other cases the gadgets are doing things the Talent can do better. The Beak, who was a doctor on Earth, is experimenting with knifeless surgery.

And there's one more major question to be answered: where did the transmatter in the arena come from? Who left it there, and why? And where did these people—as Earth-human as I—come from? The answers must somehow be related. Does the alien machine just receive, or can we make it transmit? And where will it take us? Long Harry keeps asking these questions, and wondering, and sharpening his sword.

Someday soon we'll go find out.